4

DEEP STATE

BEAR LOGAN BOOK FOUR

L.T. RYAN

For information contact:

contact@ltryan.com

http://LTRyan.com

https://www.facebook.com/JackNobleBooks

THE JACK NOBLE SERIES

The Recruit (free)
The First Deception (Prequel 1)
Noble Beginnings
A Deadly Distance
Ripple Effect (Bear Logan)
Blowback (Bear Logan)
Takedown (Bear Logan)
Deep State (Bear Logan)
Thin Line
Noble Intentions
When Dead in Greece
Noble Retribution
Noble Betrayal
Never Go Home
Beyond Betrayal (Clarissa Abbot)
Noble Judgment
Never Cry Mercy

Deadline
End Game

Receive a free copy of The Recruit by visiting http:// ltryan.com/newsletter.

1

"AFTER ALL THAT BUILDUP, YOU'RE GOING TO LEAVE ME HANGING LIKE that?"

"You know I like a good dramatic pause, Bear."

Bear could tell Jack was enjoying himself. It had been a while since they'd gotten to rib each other, and it was much better to do it in person than over the phone. Bear couldn't even bring himself to be annoyed. It was just nice to be back in the same place, like old times.

Except it wasn't like old times. Jack was still considered a terrorist-at-large, and the threat of the next World War was hanging over their heads.

"Let's go somewhere noisier," Jack said.

Bear nodded and followed Jack as they wove their way back through the crowd. Oktoberfest in Germany is better than anything you could ever experience in the United States. It's what dreams are made of. Food and women and beer and friends. Big burly men hugging each other and laughing. An atmosphere that begs you to let go of all your problems and just enjoy yourself.

And Bear was hardly seeing any of it.

He'd had his fill over the last couple of days, not that he'd ever get tired of eating and drinking. But he was starting to sober up now. He was also starting to come down from the high of seeing Jack again after so long. This whole situation with Thorne, the entire conspiracy, was beginning to feel real. He kept his head on a swivel.

Jack looked less concerned, but Bear noticed the tension in his shoulders. He was ready for anything. He probably had a weapon on him, too, despite the density of the crowd. It'd be dangerous to pull a gun out in a place like this, but if this turned into and *us or them* scenario, Bear would be glad to choose him and Jack.

He felt naked without his own weapon. He trusted Jack to cover both of them, but there was something about the weight of a weapon in the palm of his hand that made him feel secure. He made a mental note to see if Jack had a backup piece he could keep on him.

They were bumped and jostled on their way to who knows where, but Bear didn't mind. Everyone was having a good time, and for now, the threat felt like it couldn't pierce the bubble of Oktoberfest. Jack nodded at a person here or there, and Bear wondered if he was just being polite or if he had men stationed throughout the crowd in case something did go wrong.

Jack led Bear to a crowded open-air restaurant. It was packed from wall to wall, but there was a single empty table in the back corner. Bear had a feeling Jack had reserved it for them, which was confirmed when he saw Jack shake hands with the waiter, who immediately slipped his hand in his pocket.

Bear squeezed his way through the room. The other diners saw him coming and did their best to hold onto their meals before he could knock them off the table. Nobody seemed to mind, though. That was the charm of eating in a place like this. It was worth sitting elbow to elbow with your neighbors.

When they finally made it to the table, Bear took the chair opposite the bar. The man behind him had seen him coming and scooted in as far as he could. Bear nodded his thanks. He had just enough room to slide down into the chair. For his part, Jack squeezed into his own seat, which backed up against the bar. There was no way he was going to finagle anymore room for himself.

Bear felt like a sardine in a tin can, and when Jack looked up at him, he laughed until there were tears in his eyes.

"Are you happy?" Bear asked. His voice was gruff, but he was hiding a smile. "Does this bring you joy?"

"It does." Jack wiped his eyes. "I promise you I got the roomiest table in this joint. Only the best for you, Bear."

Jack's waiter friend showed up and they each ordered a beer and as much food as they could handle. Bear wasn't convinced it would all fit on the table at once, but he didn't care. It was time to load up on as much as he could while Jack filled him in.

Jack leaned forward and put his arms on the table. Bear mirrored him. The restaurant was loud with chatter and silverware clinking against plates and bowls. There was no way anyone would be able to hear them, but Bear wasn't going to take any chances. They'd keep their voices low and their eyes roaming.

"Well?" Bear asked.

"Tell me what you know."

Bear sighed but didn't fight it. Jack had already said he was having trouble figuring out where to start. Maybe this would give him a jumping off point.

"Sadie and I spoke to Thorne. He had an audio jammer, so as far as I know, everything he said was confidential."

"I told him you wouldn't believe him," Jack said. He sounded amused.

"I don't. Mostly." Bear sighed again. "I don't want to believe him, but then things started adding up."

"What did he tell you?"

Bear opened his mouth but didn't say anything until the waiter who had arrived with their beer walked away again. He took a deep pull and drank half the golden liquid down all in one go.

"He said Senator Goddard had collected state secrets and sold them to the highest bidder, including foreign powers. That's why he sent me and Sadie to Korea. We had to clean up his mess so he could keep his hands clean."

"Sounds like Thorne," Jack said, draining half his beer, too.

"Apparently Goddard had bits and pieces of information that pointed to someone within the government putting together a plan to cause the next World War." Bear couldn't keep the doubt out of his voice. "He also said you were his backup plan."

Jack didn't look proud, but he also didn't deny it. "I nearly shot him the first time he showed up face to face. After all that goddamn running around, he just waltzed right back into my life. I had a gun to his head and everything. I didn't care who would've seen me."

"What made you stop?" Bear was still trying to imagine a scenario where Jack didn't shoot first and ask questions later.

"He mentioned you and Sadie. He said something big was going on. He gave me his piece, fully loaded. Told me if I didn't believe him by the end of it, I could shoot him dead with his own gun."

"He must've been pretty convincing."

Jack's lip twitched. "Almost shot him anyway, just for the hell of it."

"He would've deserved it," Bear said, holding up his glass.

Jack knocked his beer against Bear's. "And more."

"Thorne said London was just the first domino, that more was coming. He said all of this was some nationalist bullshit, that it was all about re-establishing the United States as the strongest nation in the world."

"I bet the money helps, too," Jack said.

"*War is profitable.* That's what Thorne said."

"He's not wrong."

"The CIA thinks you're working with Thorne, Jack. They think you're a terrorist."

Jack shrugged his shoulders, like Bear had just accused him of eating the last slice of pie. "They're not wrong about the first part. I didn't set off any bombs, though."

"I know that."

"You must've had your doubts."

Bear drained the last of his beer before he answered. "I didn't know where you were, Jack. Didn't know what you were up to. I found out from Dottie that you were in London and hadn't even reached out. We were starting to connect the dots, and none of it was looking good."

Jack held up a hand. "I don't blame you. You had more faith in me than I probably deserved, especially after going radio silent."

"We both did what we had to do."

Jack nodded his head, and just like that, Bear felt the last remnants of any tension between the two of them completely disappear. They were back on track. Back to normal.

"Your turn," Bear said.

Another round of drinks and an unseemly amount of food showed up before Jack could say anything. Bear had momentarily forgotten how hungry he was, and the two of them spent the next several moments in silence, eating a little bit of everything from their plates.

"It all comes back to the Middle East," Jack said, his mouth half full of sausage.

"Doesn't it always?"

Jack tipped his head in agreement and swallowed the rest of his bratwurst. "Thorne showed me the evidence he had gathered from Goddard. The plan is to destabilize the Middle East while simultaneously coordinating attacks around the world."

"To what end? We already have our hands in that pot."

"Not like this," Jack said. "Imagine something like the Treaty of Versailles for the countries of the Middle East, where reparations come in the form of controlling their resources, their oil."

Bear couldn't help his reaction. He had a fork full of rouladen halfway to his mouth when he froze. This entire thing seemed like some crazy conspiracy theory when they had first talked to Thorne, something way beyond the scope of reality. But this made sense. This was plausible. This was a situation he could see the government trying to manipulate.

But his brain still wouldn't accept it. "Who would have the balls to do that? This would require immense coordination. You'd have to trust the people on your side with your whole life. Discretion would have to be absolute. Who would have that kind of pull?"

Jack looked Bear right in the eyes before he answered. It was another one of his damn dramatic pauses.

"What about the Director of National Intelligence?"

2

THIS TIME, BEAR ACTUALLY PUT HIS FOOD BACK DOWN ON HIS PLATE. "Come again?"

Jack wasn't so discerning. He shoved more food into his mouth before answering. "That's what Thorne's evidence was pointing toward."

Bear tried to dredge up all the information he knew about the current Director of National Intelligence. He was drawing a blank. He told Jack as much.

"His name is Mason Hughes," Jack supplied. "His track record is spotless. Honestly, he's one of the best we've had in a while. He's sharp, smart, and doesn't have a problem making tough calls. He practically came out of the womb singing 'The Star-Spangled Banner'."

"Maybe that's the problem," Bear said. "I'm damn proud of this country, but that doesn't mean it's perfect."

"From what I've gathered, Hughes is aware. He's gotten his hands dirty a few times, but he always came out on top. It always seemed to be the right call by the time all was said and done. No one ever thought less of him because of it. Definitely not the president."

"Which would have given him reason to believe something like this is the right call."

"He's probably hoping he'll get a medal by the end of it."

"Control over the Middle East and oil prices the lowest they've ever been?" Bear said. "He probably would."

"Doesn't make it right."

"No, it doesn't." Bear washed his food down with the rest of his beer. "But this is a big play. You have any idea how they're going to pull it off?"

"Some." Jack wiped his hands on a napkin and leaned over his plate. "I guarantee you that Hughes is gunning for a presidential run. He's playing this as close to the chest as he can. No one knows everything, except for him. What Thorne has gathered is as close to a complete dossier as we're ever going to get."

Bear knew this was Jack's way of telling Bear nothing was a guarantee. He didn't care. "Understood."

"There's a man named Thomas Mateo. He's some eccentric billionaire who has more money than he can count, but in between jet-setting across the world in private planes and vacationing on yachts the size of mansions, he's started spearheading an effort for green energy."

"Ironic, but how is it connected?"

"My guess is that once the Middle East has been destabilized, everyone is going to start selling. Energy companies will be worth pennies on the dollar, and Mateo has enough money to buy them all. He can convert them to green energy, bring stability back to the region and make both his and Hughes' agenda look better."

"He'll still be a monopoly. People hate monopolies."

"A green monopoly," Jack said, pointing his fork at Bear. "People are willing to pay more to support a good cause. My guess is they'll find a way to keep it cheaper for those who are on the right side of history. Mateo and Hughes will be heroes in everyone's eyes, swimming in more money and power than anyone could ever dream of."

"And no one will ever know they caused the whole thing to begin with."

Jack sat back and laughed. "I imagine that is the ultimate goal."

"You think Mateo is the weak link, don't you?"

Jack leaned back and sighed, surveying the damage he had dealt to the plates in front of him. "I do."

"What makes you say that?"

"He's not a politician or a military man. He's a big kid who grew up on Daddy's money and turned millions into billions. He's smart, but I don't think he would last under pressure. As far as I can tell, Hughes is blackmailing a lot of the people he's working with. He doesn't have anything on Mateo. He doesn't need it. Hughes just needs to keep Mateo happy and keep reminding him of all the money they're going to make."

"And you think if there's any doubt in Mateo's mind that Hughes is going to hold up his end of the bargain, Mateo will fold?"

Jack nodded. "There's also the chance that he grows a conscience, but he's already in pretty deep. He knows what Hughes is planning on doing and he agreed to it anyway."

"So, what's the next play?"

"That's what I'm trying to figure out. We need to get into contact with Mateo, set up a meeting."

"Preferably alone," Bear added.

"Preferably. I have a possible lead, but I'm not sure how it's going to play out just yet. There are a lot of wildcards here, Bear. This could get very messy, very fast. We're not taking down some random foreign contact in another country. This is back home, in the President's Cabinet."

"What do you need from me?" Bear asked.

"I need you to be my boots on the ground." Jack leaned forward, serious. "I'd do it myself, but—"

Bear held up his hand. "You're a wanted man. It'll be ten times easier for me."

"They're still watching you."

Bear waved off the comment. "I can shake them long enough to do this."

Jack pulled a cell phone from his pocket. "Take this. Go home. I'll contact you in about three days. I should have more information by then."

Bear looked down at the phone. "It's going to be hard for me to get back out of the States again if you need me. They must've noticed I've left by now."

"Whatever is going on here, it's centered in the States, even if everything else is happening out here. We have to focus on the disease, not the symptoms."

Bear knew he was right, but it didn't make him like it any better. Still, he pocketed the phone and stood up as Jack threw some bills down on the table. The waiter from earlier made his way over to them.

"Anything else I can get you, gentlemen?"

"It was great, Elias. Thank you."

"It was the least I can do," Elias said. The gratitude in his eyes made Bear think Jack had been keeping busy while he was on the run.

Elias shook both of their hands before they headed toward the door, trying their best not to upset any tables along the way. Jack led Bear outside and stood on the sidewalk, rubbing his hands together to stay warm. It was starting to get dark now. There was a chill in the air.

"You still playing a hero?" Bear asked, hooking his thumb over his shoulder back toward the restaurant.

"His brother owed a little too much money to the wrong people. I helped even the playing field. Don't worry, I got my reward for it."

Bear chuckled. "I was worried there for a minute."

"About what?"

"That you'd turned into a white knight."

It was Jack's turn to laugh. "No chance of that."

"Good to know," Bear said. "Can't have you going soft on me."

Jack laughed, but whatever he was about to say next was drowned out by an explosion so loud, it momentarily deafened Bear. The subsequent shockwave knocked them off their feet. One second he was standing, and the next he was eating concrete.

It took Bear a minute to get his bearings. The side of his face burned where it had scraped against the sidewalk. His world was blurry at the edges for a few seconds before it snapped back into crisp focus. He looked around and noticed Jack standing above him, shouting something.

"I'm okay," Bear said, allowing Jack to haul him to his feet. His voice sounded strange, like he was yelling in a wind tunnel. He tried to pop his ears, but nothing shifted. Nothing hurt either, which was a good sign, all things considered.

Bear turned to Jack and blinked the last of the blurriness from his eyes. He looked down at Jack's lips and got an idea of what he was yelling at him. It was only a few words, but it was more than enough to realize what was going on.

Explosion. Bomb. Terrorist attack.

If London was the first domino, then Munich was the second.

3

BEAR TURNED BACK TOWARD THE OKTOBERFEST ACTIVITIES AND took it all in. Smoke billowed from the center of the festival. People were screaming, running in all directions. A woman gripped her child against her chest and ran past them at full speed. She wasn't wearing any shoes and blood trickled from the side of her head. Bear hoped the kid was okay.

Jack sprinted toward the chaos. Bear cursed and followed after him. So much for not being a hero.

Any thought of walking in the other direction was immediately thrown away the second Bear saw the destruction before him. Whoever had set the bomb off made sure it was right in the middle of the main square. Bear couldn't help but wonder if it had been planted the entire time they were there, or if someone had walked forward with a six-pack of C4 and blew themselves up right alongside everything else.

It took a minute for Bear's eyes to adjust to the scene. It looked like a kid had dumped out his Lincoln Logs and Legos and left them strewn around the living room. He could only recognize bits and pieces of the stands from earlier. Everything else was just shrapnel.

As his hearing started to come back, Bear started to make out the wails of people who had been hit by the explosion or the debris. Anyone in close proximity to the bomb would be a paint smear on the ground, but those unlucky enough to have been farther away or shielded now had to deal with the repercussions.

Jack processed the scene much more quickly than Bear. He was already on his knees, taking the scarf from one woman's neck and tying it around her thigh. There was a large piece of wood embedded in the muscle. If she got help, she would be fine, but there was a chance she could bleed out before that happened. Bear walked closer.

"—not going to remove it," Jack said.

"Please," the woman cried. Tears and blood were smeared across her face. Her English was accented, but clear. "Please. Please take it out."

"I can't." Jack put a reassuring hand on her shoulder, forcing her to look directly into his eyes. "I'm not sure how close it is to the artery in your leg. If I remove it, you'll start bleeding. You have to wait until they take you to the hospital."

The woman started crying harder, but she nodded her head as she looked away from her wound.

"Stay here," Jack said. "They'll come for you. You're going to be okay."

The woman closed her eyes and sobbed. Jack stood up and looked from Bear to the rest of the wreckage. "Go right. I'll go left. Help as many as you can. We don't have much time."

Bear didn't question the order. He lumbered into ground zero, being careful to avoid tramping on anything that looked like it had once belonged to a person. Even if it was a single finger or a piece of an earlobe, it might be the only piece of evidence that someone had died here. He didn't want to take that away from a grieving family looking for answers.

In less than five steps, Bear came across a man holding a hand to his neck. He was covered in blood and his eyes already looked glassy. He perked up a little bit when he saw Bear and reached his hand out for him.

Bear didn't hesitate. He had been in enough combat situations to come to two conclusions instantly. One, this man was going to die. A piece of shrapnel had probably sliced open his neck. Anywhere else and he probably would've lived. Unlike the woman, the debris hadn't lodged itself in there to stop the bleeding. Or maybe the man had pulled it out. Either way, it was only a matter of time.

The other conclusion Bear had come to was that this man knew he was dying and didn't want to be alone. Sometimes it's easier to accept your death if you have someone there with you while you make your way out the door. Even if it's just a stranger.

Bear took the man's hand and gripped it hard. He sat him up, and the man's hand slipped from his neck. It was a nasty wound. Bear would've been able to see inside his neck if it weren't for all the blood.

The man tried to speak, but it just came out as a gurgle.

"It's okay," Bear said. He kept his voice quiet, but firm. "It's okay. You're safe now. Just relax."

Another gurgle. Panic in the eyes.

Bear looked down at the man's chest. He was wearing a small, golden cross. Bear hoped he spoke English.

"It's okay," Bear said again. "This next part is easy. You're in good hands now. It's time to rest."

There was one last gurgle and Bear saw the light slip from the man's eyes. It was amazing how different it was, watching the life drain from the eyes of someone you'd killed and someone who happened to die in front of you. Bear didn't particularly like either one of them, but he especially didn't like the helplessness that was settling in his chest.

Bear laid the man's head back and stood up, ignoring the sticky blood on his hands. He took a few steps forward and noticed another person on the ground. It was an older woman, her face slack and her body unmoving. Bear knew she was dead, but he checked her pulse any way. Quiet. He moved on.

A few people had hauled themselves to their feet now, stumbling forward, gripping bloody limbs. Bear ignored those who could walk. They'd find their way out of the wreckage on their own. He was more concerned about those who were trapped. Those who were about to give up.

A soft crying sounded from his right, and he made a beeline for it. There was a tarp still burning, giving off a putrid scent of burning plastic. He choked on the fumes, but when a whimper sounded from the other side, he stepped closer.

"Help." The voice was weak. Young. "Please."

Bear sidestepped the tarp and peered behind it. There was a small girl, maybe sixteen or seventeen, seated against a concrete wall. She gripped her left leg with both hands. Her right arm was badly burned. There were even some pieces of the tarp melted to her skin.

"Did you see what happened?" Bear asked, kneeling beside her.

"There was a bomb," the girl said. She was American. Her voice was distant, like she was still trying to understand her own words. "People started running everywhere. Someone pushed me down and then I just felt my leg crack."

Her voice caught, and Bear took the opportunity to speak. "I need to see if it's completely broken or not. It's going to hurt, but it'll tell me whether or not I can move you."

The girl looked into Bear's eyes like she was searching for what kind of person he was. After a few seconds, she gritted her teeth and nodded. Bear wasn't sure he deserved what she had found there, but he wasn't going to argue. If he saved at least one person today, it would be enough.

"My name is Bear, by the way."

The girl choked out a laugh. "Really?"

"Really."

"Amber."

"It's nice to meet you, Amber." Bear gently pushed her hands out of the way. "Just bear with me a moment, okay? The pain will spike, but it'll dull down shortly."

"Bear with you?" Amber said. "Is that supposed to be funny?"

Bear didn't answer her. Instead, he ran his hand down the front of her leg. When he got to an area that was bruised and swollen, she hissed through her teeth and groaned. He then ran his hands up the side of her legs to see if anything was badly out of place.

"The good news is it's not badly broken," Bear said. "I don't think your leg was crushed. It could end up being a clean break."

Amber nodded her head and swallowed. She didn't look at her arm directly, but she did point to it with her chin. "And this?"

Bear didn't want to lie to her. She seemed like a tough kid, even if she was scared out of her mind. "It's pretty badly burned. They'll need to remove the plastic that's still attached to you. Does it hurt?"

"Like a motherfucker," she said.

Bear almost laughed. He cracked a smile instead. "That's a good sign. It might just be a second-degree burn. No nerve damage."

"How do you know all this?"

"Military," Bear said. Amber nodded like that was the only

answer she needed. Maybe she was an army brat and that was why she was in Germany. Bear didn't ask.

Bear grabbed two straight pieces of wooden sticks and found some scrap tent fabric and fashioned a splint around her leg. When he tied it tightly, she hissed and groaned again, but didn't complain.

"I'm going to lift you now and take you someplace where it's easier to get to you, okay?"

"Okay." Amber's voice sounded a little stronger now, a little more hopeful.

Bear did his best not to jostle her too much, but he knew moving her was going to be painful. Amber cried out but told him to keep going. So he did. He walked Amber back to the woman with the piece of wood in her leg and set her down against a low wall. Amber breathed through the pain, keeping her eyes closed. The woman reached out for the girl and gripped her hand. The two of them remained silent.

Bear was about to make his way back into the fray when he realized he had been hearing sirens in the distance. They were much closer now. Jack emerged from the wreckage, blood-spattered and sweating.

"We need to go," he said. He looked at the two women at his feet and turned back to Bear. "We did what we could."

"There's gotta be dozens more people in there," Bear said. He felt like he'd done nothing but watch people die.

Jack shook his head. "The cops are coming. They'll want statements. Pictures. Evidence. If our faces are anywhere near this, it's just going to make things worse. This wasn't an accident, Bear. It wasn't coincidence."

Bear knew he was right. Still, it didn't make it any easier. "Shit."

"Emergency responders are almost here. We did what we could. It's better than nothing."

Bear looked beyond Jack. He could just make out a few people strewn here or there. He didn't know whether they were dead or alive, but he knew Jack was right. There was nothing else they could do.

Bear took one last look at Amber. She looked back, confusion and pain plastered across her face with the blood and soot. She clutched her leg with both her hands and whispered, "Thank you, Bear."

Bear nodded. Then he turned around and walked away, slipping into the darkness with Jack, knowing that one way or another, this hadn't been an accident. Someone knew they were in Germany. They had wanted to either catch Jack and Bear in the bombing, or pin it on them entirely.

4

THREE DAYS LATER, BEAR FOUND HIMSELF IN CHICAGO, WONDERING whether Amber and the other woman had gotten the help they needed. He still felt guilty about leaving them there, but he and Jack had no choice. They'd barely made it out of the city and past the blockade as it was. If they had waited even a minute or two longer, they would've been stuck in Germany, or worse—in custody.

After leaving Munich, Jack and Bear went in separate directions. They parted with few words and no information about where either one of them was going. For his part, Bear found a change of clothes and the cheapest hostel he could. He showered, took care of the scrape on his face, and slept for a handful of hours. It wasn't even light out by the time he was on a plane back to the United States.

He was certain someone would be waiting for him at the airport when he landed. He knew that would be the case if he went directly back to New York or Atlanta, so he chose to fly into Charlotte. When he deplaned, it took all his willpower not to sprint to the exit. Instead, he took his time and diligently kept his head about him. No one in the airport seemed to be there for a reason other than to get where they needed to go.

After that, he rented a car and made his way north. As far as he could tell, the roads were clear. There were no indications he was being watched, but he knew he was. Hughes or whoever was working for him would send out the best of the best to keep an eye on Jack and, by extension, Bear. So, even though Bear didn't spot a tail, he acted like he had one, getting on and off the highway, taking the long way back to New York, and stopping off at a little-used apartment he kept stocked for situations such as these.

Bear left the car in one borough and hopped on a train to another. He walked a few blocks in one direction, took a side street, and then started walking in the opposite direction. Shaking a tail was hard when you didn't know who it was, but Bear did everything he could to make his route as chaotic as possible.

By the time he had made it to the apartment, he was exhausted. He collapsed on the couch and slept for close to twelve hours.

The only thing that woke him up was a single text from Jack. All it said was *Lady of the Lake in the tallest tower*. It didn't take long for Bear to figure out. He and Jack had some property in Chicago, the City by the Lake. It wasn't exactly the tallest building in the skyline, but they had a business there called Camelot Ltd. They owned the top few floors and rented the rest out. It'd been a while since either one of them were there, but Bear kept close tabs on it.

So, Bear showered, changed his clothes again, and hopped on another plane.

With his paranoia at an all-time high, Bear took extensive evasive maneuvers to ensure that whoever was following him had no idea where he was headed. Jack would've laughed, but Bear didn't care. It was too quiet. That told him that Hughes, if he did know about Bear's recent trip abroad, was waiting until the opportune moment to make his move.

Bear didn't want to give him even a single opening.

By the time he stood outside the office building, looking up at the glassy façade and shaded windows, Bear had convinced himself Jack had been compromised. He had only heard from him once, that one text message, and the instructions hadn't been detailed or specific.

Bear had tried calling the number a few times, but it was out of service. Jack had likely sent the message and then immediately destroyed the burner he had used. That was what they had always done, and yet something felt off to Bear.

So, he scouted the area. He watched the building. Hours passed and no one came in or out. No one suspicious wandered up and down the sidewalk. They were far enough away from downtown Chicago that it was fairly quiet, but close enough that the traffic was constant . No one passed by twice. No one gave him a second look.

Bear was about to try Jack one last time when the phone rang in his hands. He swiped it on before the first ring ended.

"It's me," Jack said from the other end. His voice was tinged with the lightest touch of static. "You there?"

"Yeah." Relief flooded through Bear. It must've sounded in his voice.

"You okay, Big Man?"

"I'm already tired of this shit. It feels like my head's been on a swivel for months."

"Good. Keep it that way. We can't afford to make any mistakes."

"You been watching the news?"

Jack sighed. The static hit a little harder. "Yeah."

Bear nodded, even though Jack couldn't see it. There was a lot he wanted to say, like how a hundred people had been confirmed dead but they were still sifting through body parts. About how it seemed like someone knew Jack had been there and that's why they chose Munich. About how their pictures hadn't gone up anywhere, but that it felt like it was just a matter of time.

But, especially, Bear wanted to talk about the handful of Americans that had died and how Hughes would be all over it. He'd get to be the hero and take Jack out of the equation at the same time. He doubted Jack was any more worried than he ever was, but this situation was clearly taking a toll on both of them.

Instead, Bear just looked up at the building in front of him and asked, "What am I going to find inside?"

"Information, I hope. Fourteenth floor. Green means go."

"Take care of yourself."

"You too, Big Man."

Bear pocketed the phone and took one last look up and down the road. It was clear of any traffic, pedestrian or otherwise. Now was the time to make his move. Bear had no way of knowing what was inside.

But there was only one way to find out.

5

BEAR TOOK HIS TIME ENTERING THE BUILDING. HE WALKED UP THE street, crossed at the crosswalk, and then back down to the front door. There was no doorman, and Bear couldn't remember if they had made that choice on purpose or not. Either way, it made his job easier for now.

The entryway was fairly basic. This wasn't one of the fancy buildings in downtown Chicago. It was well-used but well-maintained, if not a little dated. There was no receptionist either. Instead, a golden directory shone with his reflection. He scanned through the list of businesses that rented from them but didn't recognize any of the names until he got to Camelot Ltd. They took up floors fourteen through eighteen.

Bear noted the distinct lack of cameras in the lobby, which made him think they had chosen not to station a doorman at the entrance. This was the kind of building you could disappear into pretty easily. He remembered a basement with a separate stairwell for an easy exit. Maybe that was the whole reason they had bought the building to begin with.

Bear crossed the lobby and quietly pushed the door open to the stairwell. It was slightly off-white, but relatively clean. One of the lights had only a single bulb working . Still, it was quiet, which meant most everyone upstairs was probably at their desk. And, considering the building was full of unrelated companies, nobody would look at him twice, wondering why he was there.

Taking the steps two at a time, Bear huffed it up six flights before gingerly opening the door and poking his head into the hallway. There wasn't a soul in sight, but he could hear the quiet murmur of chatter interspersed with phones ringing. He exited the stairwell and jabbed the button for the elevator.

Bear didn't see another person on his way up. He started to wonder how many people were using the building anymore. Maybe they were all diligent workers. Maybe they actually liked their jobs.

He chuckled to himself.

With a *ding*, Bear arrived on the fifteenth floor. He thought again about how Jack would've made fun of him for being so cautious, but Bear didn't care. Even Jack said he didn't know what he would find once he got inside. Better safe than sorry.

Bear stepped outside the elevator and listened. This floor was dead quiet. He couldn't hear anything but the faint sound of beeping in the distance. He turned to the stairwell and crept down the stairs to the fourteenth floor, wishing he had a weapon of some sort. They usually kept a hideaway gun at every location they owned. Bear just had to find it.

When he got to the fourteenth-floor landing, Bear noticed the door was cracked open a few inches. The linoleum floor was dusty past the threshold, except for a pair of footprints leading in and out. They were much too small for Jack, and Bear suspected they may have belonged to a woman.

Bear slipped through the door and took in his surroundings.

Like floor six, there was a singular hallway with just two doors lining the hall. Unlike the other floor, however, there was an umbrella stand sitting outside the door. A bright yellow umbrella sat inside. Bear rolled his eyes. He had wished for a weapon, but maybe he should've been a little more specific.

Ask and you shall receive.

Bear grabbed the umbrella and weighed it in his hand. It was one of those huge, well-made ones that might actually do some damage in a fight. It wasn't going to stop any bullets, but it would give him some extra reach in some hand-to-hand combat.

The fourteenth floor was as quiet as the one above it, but he could hear the faint ringing of phones below him. He sifted through the sounds and concluded that he was alone on this floor. Still, it was better not to take any chances.

Bear gripped the doorknob in front of him and twisted it open. The door swung forward, and he noticed the footprints continued inside. The room was limited in furnishings, just a rusted metal desk and a cork board hanging on the wall. There were about a dozen things hanging from it, but he ignored that for now.

On the other end of the room was another door. He crossed the office space and turned the doorknob there as well. If someone was lying in wait for him, they'd be inside. He swung this door open more forcefully and stepped out of the line of sight. No shots rang out. No one charged forward. No one told him to freeze and that he was under arrest.

Bear cleared this room as well, spotting a safe sitting in the corner. There was a bathroom across the room but the door had been pulled off and set against the wall. Bear checked in there too, just in case. Empty. The entire floor was deserted.

He returned to the safe and got it open on the second try. Inside, he found a Glock 19, a spare magazine, a box of rounds, and a few thousand in cash. The perfect welcoming present for arriving in a new city. He felt the relief wash over him now that he finally had a weapon in his hand again. This entire situation seemed a little less dire.

Bear walked back to the main office. He smudged his footprints along the way, but kept the other ones intact. When he got to the bulletin board, he ignored everything but the slip of paper tacked into the cork with a green push pin. *Green means go.*

Scribbled on the slip of paper was a phone number written in blue ink. It wasn't Jack's handwriting as far as he could tell. And even though it was just a series of numbers, there was a certain flourish to them that made Bear think it was a woman. Perhaps the same person who had left the footprints?

At this point, Bear had two choices. He could either call the number directly or call someone who would be able to at least give him some idea of what he would be getting into if he went with option one. He elected for the latter.

And he had the perfect person in mind.

6

BEAR EXITED THE BUILDING THE SAME WAY HE ENTERED IT: DOWN TO the sixth floor in the elevator and then through the stairwell until he landed outside. He didn't look back as he crossed the road and headed toward downtown. It'd probably be another several years before he set foot inside those offices again. Maybe more.

Bear kept walking until he found a decent-looking restaurant with outside seating. It was November, which meant Chicago was already whipping through fall and heading straight for winter. It also meant he'd be able to have a private conversation on the patio.

The waiter, a young kid with long, blond hair, quirked an eyebrow at him when he asked if the tables outside were still available, but he nodded his head and led Bear to a seat in the corner. Bear had a view of the whole outdoor area along with the street traffic. It was perfect.

He waited until his cup of coffee and sandwich arrived before calling his contact. He was normally cautious as it was, but Brandon was especially particular about who called him and where they were doing it from. Bear knew that within three seconds of him reaching out, Brandon would know exactly where he was located. Probably knew what kind of sandwich he was eating, too.

Two full rings sounded before the line clicked over. There was no noise on the other end, but Bear knew he was there. "It's me," he said.

"Bear." Brandon always seemed to sigh with relief when he answered, like he wouldn't be convinced of who it was until they spoke. He was a little on the paranoid side, but that's what made him so good at what he did. "What can I do for you, my man?"

"I have a number I'd like to run. I want to know who it belongs to. Everything you've got on them, I need to hear about it."

There were a couple clicks on Brandon's end before he answered. Probably inspecting just how much mustard was on Bear's turkey sandwich. "Who gave you the number?"

"Jack."

Brandon laughed. "I doubt I'll be able to find anything on it."

"I'm desperate," Bear said. "Don't have a whole lot of leads otherwise."

"All right, we'll give it a try."

Bear rattled off the number to Brandon, who read it back. After Bear confirmed he had it right, the other end of the line was filled with the sound of keystrokes. A few clicks of the mouse interrupted the monotony. Bear waited patiently for five minutes. His sandwich was untouched.

"It's not looking good," Brandon said. "Jack knows how to stay off the grid. He knows how to hide his tracks."

"Yeah, I know." Bear knew that better than anyone, especially after recent events.

"I have a couple more tricks to try. Why don't you try to enjoy your lunch? I'll call you back in ten."

Bear chuckled and hung up. He dug into his sandwich with gusto, draining his coffee and asking for another when the waiter came around to check on him. It was chilly, but the coffee mixed well with the adrenaline in his bloodstream. He just hoped he'd be able to get a decent night's sleep at some point.

Just as Bear was washing down the rest of his sandwich with his second cup of coffee, his phone rang. It was an unknown number, but Bear picked it up anyway. It could only be one of two people, and he had a pretty good idea which one it was.

"Me again," Brandon said. There was laughter in his voice.

"What'd you find out?"

"Did a couple different kinds of searches. The number bounces around a lot, keeps changing every time I try. There's really no way to track exactly where it's coming from. Definitely a burner. No search came back with a name."

"So, it's a dead end then?"

"Not exactly." Brandon was clearly chuckling now. "I tried one more thing. State of the art technology. Really is pretty hard to get around this one."

"What did you do?"

"I called the number."

Bear tried to keep the annoyance out of his voice. "And? What happened?"

"A woman answered."

"A woman?" Bear asked. Could she be the owner of the footprints in the office? "What did she say?"

"She said hello a couple times. American accent. She sounded cute."

Bear couldn't keep the growl out of his voice now. "Why are you laughing?"

"Nothing, nothing." Brandon was starting to lose it. "I just keep imagining Jack setting you up."

"Setting me up?"

"Yeah." Another chuckle. "I think Jackie boy is trying to set you up on a date, Big Man."

AFTER UNCEREMONIOUSLY HANGING up on Brandon, Bear ordered a final cup of coffee. He sat back in his seat and stared at the phone, like he thought the mystery woman might call him first. After the check came, Bear paid it and dialed the number. There was no time like the present.

Right on cue, the woman answered. "Hello?"

Bear remained silent. Brandon was right. She was American – and she did sound cute. Her voice was high but strong and clear.

"Listen, creep, either say something disgusting or stop calling me."

Bear choked on his coffee. He was right about the strong part. She sounded like a firecracker.

He weighed his words. He wasn't sure how secure this line was. "I think we have a friend in common."

"Oh," she said. "You must be Bear."

"No names."

"Right, sorry." Bear could hear her swallow even over the phone. "I've been expecting your call."

Bear decided he would figure out what that meant later. "Where are you located?"

"Chicago, downtown, in—"

"Good," Bear said, cutting her off. He didn't need more detail than that. "We need to talk in person."

"Okay." There was the noise of papers being shuffled and drawers opening and closing. "When? Where?"

"Millennium Park. As soon as you can."

"It's going to be crowded there. Are you sure you—"

"More people means more privacy. No one will pay us any attention."

"Right. Got it. Okay." There was the click of a door on the other end. "I'm heading there now. How will I know it's you?"

Bear chuckled. "You'll know."

7

BEAR TOOK A TAXI TO MILLENNIUM PARK AND MADE A BEELINE FOR Cloud Gate, aka the Bean. Chances were high that's exactly where the woman would choose to meet. It was crowded, just like she said it would be, but that allowed even someone like Bear to disappear in the crowd.

He did a lap around the monument before finding the corner of a picnic table and opening up a map of Chicago he stole from the back of the taxicab. He already knew the city fairly well, but it was the best way to watch the crowd in his peripheral vision without appearing suspicious.

Bear looked up every few minutes to take a better look at his surroundings. Everyone was enjoying the crisp, clear day. Kids were running around the monument while parents took pictures and talked about what they were going to do with the rest of their day. Couples kissed and snuggled closer on the benches. Very few people were by themselves.

That's why he spotted her so quickly. Not that it was hard. She wore a bright yellow jacket and had long, raven hair. She had a messenger bag swinging off one shoulder and her phone in one hand. She stood close to the Bean and looked around. Her eyes passed right over Bear two or three times.

For his part, Bear waited. For ten minutes, he monitored her along with the crowd. She didn't speak to anyone else. Didn't look in anyone else's direction. No one approached her or passed by her too closely. She was alone. But that didn't mean she wasn't being watched. It didn't mean Bear wasn't being watched, either.

After ten minutes, Bear pulled out his phone and texted her that he was there. She looked down and up again, searching the crowd in earnest. She walked a full circle around Cloud Gate twice before expanding her radius and making her way through the crowd around the tables. She walked right by him.

Bear folded his map and tucked it and the phone back in his pocket. He trailed behind her, but it wasn't hard staying out of sight. She never looked behind her. Not even once. Bear sighed. He wondered how Jack knew her and why he was working with someone so green.

After ten more minutes, the woman was growing visibly frustrated. She texted him at least two more times, but he didn't bother looking at what she said. When she stopped and put her phone away, Bear knew she was ready to give up. He passed by her shoulder, close enough that she would be able to hear him.

"Follow me."

He didn't bother looking back. She either would or wouldn't. He preferred the former, but if it ended up being the latter, he'd wait for Jack to call him and they'd figure out what to do next.

Bear walked until he reached Crown Fountain. Then he stepped off the path and leaned up against one of the trees, surveying the crowd in front of him. The woman was a few paces behind him in that godawful yellow coat. She stalked right up to him and crossed her arms over her chest.

"You're not really good at keeping a low profile, are you?" he asked, pointing at her jacket.

"Are you Bear? Did Jack send you?"

Bear didn't bother confirming his identity. "Who are you and how do you know Jack?"

The woman sighed and pinched the bridge of her nose. She looked tired. "My name is Cara Bishop. I'm an investigative journalist. I was introduced to Jack through various backchannels."

"That's not very specific."

"It's not like you're offering up a fountain of information," she said.

That was fair, but he wasn't going to let her know that. "How old are you?"

Cara scrunched up her face. "Twenty-six. Why is that relevant?"

"You're younger than I expected."

"I'm very good at my job," she retorted.

"Jack wouldn't keep you on hand if you weren't."

Bear scanned the crowd again. He didn't like this setup. He certainly didn't like getting information from someone who could turn around and put his whole life story in the newspaper if he let the wrong detail slip

But it's not like he had much choice. "What do you know?"

"Hang on." Cara put up a hand and looked him up and down. "This isn't a free exchange. Jack said you could help me. How do I know you'll keep up your end of the bargain?"

"You don't," Bear said, "but I'll tell you what I can."

Cara held her squint for a few more seconds before reaching into her bag and pulling out a small notebook. "Everything I have is in here."

"A notebook? Isn't that a little...outdated?" Bear wasn't great with technology, but at least he hadn't written down information about the biggest scandal in U.S. history in a notebook he could've gotten at Wal-Mart for under a dollar.

"It's for you," she said, handing it over. "Jack told me to give you a copy of everything. I didn't know how you were with computers, so I elected for something a little easier, just in case."

Bear snatched the notebook out of her hand and tucked it into his back pocket. "Start from the beginning. I want to know everything."

Cara tucked a piece of hair behind her ear. She leveled one more look at him and then crossed her arms over her chest. "I was tasked with doing a profile on a man named Senator Thomas Goddard. It was just supposed to be filler. He had been climbing the ranks. My newspaper wanted me to talk to him, figure out what made him tick."

"Give him more exposure and possibly gain some favor with him?"

She quirked a smile. "You're not as dumb as you look."

"If I had a nickel every time I heard that."

Cara laughed. It was soft and high. Her eyes crinkled at the corners. "I was in his office when he took a phone call. His entire demeanor changed like *that*." She snapped her fingers. "One minute he was jovial, down-to-earth, even a little dorky."

"And the next?"

Her face took on a somber look. "He was all hard lines and angles. The whole atmosphere of the room changed. I felt claustrophobic, like he was too big and too close. His voice had this edge to it. Honestly, it scared me."

"What was the phone call about?"

"He only said a few things. I heard him say something about Costa Rica. Something about passing a bill in the Senate. Then he said he'd deal with it later. He hung up, and just like that, he was back."

"Just like before?"

"Almost. There was something in his eyes. Or maybe I'd finally seen something I couldn't unsee." She rubbed her arms, like the memory had given her a chill. "I wrapped up the interview as quickly as I could."

"And then you started digging into him." Bear was impressed, but he couldn't help thinking she had made the wrong call. She was too young, too green to get mixed up in all of this.

"I pulled everything I could on him, from the minute he was born to the day I conducted the interview. I told the paper it was research for my piece. No one questioned it."

"And what did you find out?"

"Goddard was smart but he wasn't too careful. He'd take a meeting here and there, and then a few months down the line, one of the obstacles in his way would suddenly disappear. I never had any hard evidence, but it was pretty clear he was blackmailing people."

"Did you run the profile?"

Cara laughed again, but this one was harsh. "Obviously. I didn't have a choice."

"But you never stopped digging?"

She shook her head. "I had to be more careful. I tried to do a follow-up piece, but the paper decided it wasn't worth my time. They assigned me other tasks. I worked on them during the day, but at night, it was right back to Goddard."

"Did anyone ever pay you a visit? Did anyone ever reach out to you?"

Cara hesitated for a fraction of a second, but Bear noticed it. "No."

He lifted an eyebrow, but didn't press her. "What was your big break?"

"Goddard's death. He died mysteriously in Costa Rica. I

thought it was all over after that, but there was no power vacuum. Things went on, business as usual."

"You think someone else stepped into his shoes?"

"There's no other explanation for it. Everyone should've breathed a sigh of relief. They should've tried reversing some of his most recent proposals. But they didn't. That tells me someone was pulling Goddard's strings, and once he was out of the picture, they just chose someone else."

"Do you know who?"

She shook her head, her raven hair swinging back and forth. "I never got that far."

"Why?"

"Because I landed in the middle of something else, something bigger."

"What's that?"

"The reason why you're here, Bear." She cracked a smile. "I found out the Director of National Intelligence, Mason Hughes, is getting his hands dirtier and dirtier every day."

8

"How?" Bear asked.

"What do you mean how?"

"I mean, how did you find this out?"

Cara scoffed. "I tell you a member of the President's Cabinet is corrupt, and you ask me how I know?"

"You haven't told me anything I don't already know," Bear said. "I need sources. I need evidence. If you can't provide that, you're of no use to me."

Cara's face flushed with anger. "I wouldn't be here if I didn't have information to corroborate what I'm telling you."

"Then let's hear it."

"Hughes has been playing chess while everyone else has been playing checkers. He's been putting pieces into place for years without anyone being the wiser."

"Except you?"

Cara rolled her eyes. "I told you, I'm good at my job. But not that good. I've had help. It took a long time to get this far. I'm still missing some pretty big pieces. But I *know* there's something here. I know there's a thread that needs pulling."

"And you think you're going to be the one to do it?"

"Me?" She laughed. "Hell no. Believe it or not, I value my life. This is way bigger than me. I want to do the right thing, but I don't want to die because of it."

"That's the first sensible thing you've said all day."

"I'm aware." Cara brushed her hair out of her face. The anger had left red blotches across her cheeks. "Hughes has been talking to a man named Mateo. He's some bigshot millionaire who's trying to convince Congress to go green. He's made plenty of trips to Washington, particularly to see Hughes. But Hughes is the Director of National Intelligence. Why are they meeting behind closed doors?"

"Old friends?" Bear guessed.

"Not that I can tell. They started talking about a year ago. Since then Mateo has been making major moves, selling older companies and acquiring new ones. He's been purchasing patents for technology related to green energy."

"That doesn't seem strange on paper."

"No, it's doesn't. But you want to know what does? The fact that the number of green pieces of legislation has nearly tripled in the last twelve months."

Bear shrugged. "People are becoming more environmentally friendly."

"Goddard was all gung-ho about a pipeline that would've made the U.S. less dependent on foreign powers with an oil supply. It's dead in the water. Just like *that*." She snapped her fingers.

"Pipelines are expensive. That kind of shit happens every day."

Cara groaned. She took a step closer. If Bear were a smaller man, he might've been intimidated. "Every single one of these things looks like nothing on paper. They look like everyday occurrences. But once you start tracking them, you can see a clear pattern. And it points to Hughes and Mateo."

"Is that everything?" Bear asked.

Her eyebrows knit together. "What do you mean *is that everything*? Yes, that's everything. It's more than enough to start digging through."

"I don't dig," Bear said. He reached into his pocket and pulled out the SIM card in his phone. Then, he snapped the phone in half and held it out to Cara.

She took it, her mouth hanging open for a few seconds while she processed what it meant. "What are you doing?"

"We're done here. You haven't given me anything I don't already know. I appreciate the notebook. I'll go through it to see if there's something that catches my eye. I might be able to lean on someone who can get me close to Mateo."

"You can't just leave me here," Cara said. The shock was starting to wear off, overtaken by anger. Her cheeks flushed again.

"Yes, I can." Bear pushed off the tree and started to walk away. "I'm sorry, Ms. Bishop. There's nothing I can do for you."

"You son of a bitch," Cara said.

There was enough venom in her voice that Bear stopped and turned around. She gripped the pieces of his phone so tightly that her knuckles had turned white. She stalked toward him, and if there wasn't such a deadly serious look in her eyes, he might have laughed at this small woman walking up to him like she could take him down with just a single look.

For a second, he thought maybe she could.

"You son of a bitch," she repeated. "I've risked everything for this story. My career. My *life*. I know you think I'm just a young kid who doesn't know what she's doing, but I get it, okay? I understand what this means. Hughes and Mateo are only the tip of the iceberg, and if this is just the beginning, I don't want to see what it looks like when we cross the finish line."

"You and me both."

"Then help me." Cara's voice was less shrill now, but she still said it with force. "I can't just drop this, Bear. Not when I know I could have done something to stop it."

"We don't have any evidence. We don't have a way of getting to Mateo without turning the spotlight on us."

Cara looked sheepish now. "Actually," she said, licking her lips nervously, "that's not entirely true."

"So, you were holding out on me."

She took a deep breath. "I have a source."

"A source?"

She nodded.

"Who is it?"

"Someone important. Someone in the White House."

"How do you know someone in the White House?"

"I don't," she said. "They reached out to me."

"Who is it?" Bear asked again.

"I don't want to tell you that."

Bear threw his hands up. "I can't help you if you're not honest with me."

"I am being honest with you." Cara jabbed a finger in his direction. "I'm telling you everything I know except this. I'm not going to give you the name of my source. Not yet. Not until I know I can trust you."

"You trust Jack, don't you?"

"To an extent. But you're not Jack."

"Yeah, no shit." Jack's biggest source was a kid with dreams of winning a Pulitzer. He wouldn't have hung everything on her. "Who is it?"

"I'm not telling you."

"*Then I can't help you,*" he repeated.

"Bear," she said. Her voice was raw now, trembling. Maybe she'd win an Oscar alongside that Pulitzer. Or maybe she was really that scared. She should be. "Please. I'm willing to let you walk away over this. I'm not telling you who it is. If this is as far as we go, then so be it. But I want to keep going. Jack told me I can trust you. He brought us together for a reason. If nothing else, just trust me on this one, okay?"

Everything inside Bear was screaming at him to walk away.

He didn't.

"What do they know?"

"Not what. Who. They can get us a meeting with Mateo."

"Okay."

"Okay?" The fire was completely gone from her now. "What do you mean, 'Okay'?"

"Exactly what it sounds like." He turned around. "I'll be in touch."

"What?" Cara reached for his arm, but one look made her drop her hand back to her side. "You're leaving, just like that?"

"Lay low for a few days—"

"No, I—"

"*Lay low,*" Bear growled. "We can't be seen together. I need to get my footing. If we're meeting Mateo, I need to get up to speed. Reach out to your contact."

"And then what?"

"Then we start making moves."

When Bear walked away this time, Cara Bishop had the good sense not to follow.

9

STUDYING THAT MAP IN MILLENNIUM PARK WAS A SMART PLAY after all.

After Bear made sure Cara hadn't followed him, he walked down State Street until he found the Chicago Public Library's main branch, the Harold Washington Library Center. He made his way through various rooms and bookstacks until he found a table lined with computers. The monitors hummed with energy, but otherwise, the place was dead quiet. Perfect.

Bear sat down and placed Cara's notebook in front of him. Only the first ten pages were filled in, but her handwriting was tight and neat. There was a ton of information here. He knew most of it, but the few names and places he didn't recognize were enough to get him started.

Although Bear told Cara he didn't dig, he wasn't opposed to research duty once in a while. He could've called up Brandon and had him track down the people he hadn't heard of before, but he tried not to tap into that resource too often. Brandon got a little paranoid if you contacted him too frequently.

Besides, the change of pace was nice.

It was fairly brainless work. As great a resource as the internet was, some people didn't have an online presence. Without a police directory to go through, there was only so much he could do. Tracking down some of these names would require a little leg work in the end.

But it wasn't until he reached the part that concerned Mateo that Bear really started to get interested. He did a quick search for the billionaire online, but didn't come across anything damning. As far as the general public was aware, Mateo was an altruistic if eccentric entrepreneur. Those that knew him spoke highly of his philanthropy but didn't mind poking a little fun at his crazy ideas, like flying electric cars and living in satellite hotels in orbit around the Earth.

What did catch Bear's eye, however, was one of Mateo's frequent collaborators. It was a man named Mitch Waller. He was a tech guru who had fallen on hard times. He wasn't a billionaire by any stretch of the imagination, but he still lived the billionaire life—all thanks to Mateo. Turns out, they were also childhood friends.

Waller had specialized in technology relating to artificial intelligence until—big surprise—about a year ago, when he switched over to green technology. He and Mateo had made a big deal about it, opening their own lab and promising advancement every year they were in operation. By the end of 2007, they were pioneers in the field. By November 2008, the green tech world was looking to them for the next big thing.

But all had been quiet over the last few months.

Waller, typically more public and sociable than the awkward and arrogant Mateo, was nowhere to be seen. His social accounts were consistently updated, but the statuses were vague and never featured current pictures. Supporters said he was busy developing important, world-changing technology. Conspiracy theorists said there had been government interference.

Bear was the last one to give much credit to the conspiracy theorists, but it didn't mean they were wrong. There might not be government interference like they suspected, but it didn't mean Hughes wasn't putting pressure on Waller—and by extension, Mateo—to follow through with their promises.

Bear didn't notice the tall, thin, elderly woman until she tapped him on the shoulder. He looked up at her, his eyes blurry from staring at the screen. How long had he been there?

"There's a two-hour limit on the computers, dear," she said. She looked kind, but she had a force to her voice that made him want to obey her every command.

"I'm sorry, ma'am. I'll wrap this up and get out of your hair."

She smiled and patted him on the shoulder. "Thank you, young man. I didn't want to drag you out of here by your ear."

Bear chuckled as she walked away, turning back to the computer and clearing his search history.

It wasn't much, but it was enough of a lead to look into. He knew Cara wouldn't be happy if he didn't fill her in on the details, but he had no intention of involving her any further. She had her whole life ahead of her. This kind of story could be a career-maker, but that was only if she made it out undetected. She needed to keep her head down. There'd be another story.

Bear pocketed the notebook and nodded at the elderly librarian as he exited back the way he had come. The chilly Chicago air met him at the exit, and he shoved his hands in his pockets. His research told him that Waller, unlike Mateo, had a house in Chicago.

Chances are Waller probably wasn't home. He could be away, with or without Mateo, doing research or shaking hands with the men and women who paid his bills. Or, maybe the conspiracy theorists were right. He could be locked up in his lab, doing whatever he did that got all those tech junkies so excited.

But if he was home, Bear would have plenty to talk to him about. He needed to get in with Mateo, and Waller was the perfect opening. If he could convince Waller that Mateo was in trouble and Bear was in a position to help, he could probably get a meeting with him.

Bear hailed a cab and gave the driver directions to Waller's suburban neighborhood. He wasn't exactly lowkey when it came to giving his address out. Between the house parties and the media constantly biting at his heels, most people would know where he lived if they spent more than five minutes searching for it.

Still, Bear elected to be dropped off a few streets over to avoid any unwanted questions from the cabbie. He handed the man a hundred-dollar bill and promised twice that if he stuck around. The man smiled and nodded, then pulled a book from his glove compartment and settled in.

Bear got out of the car and shoved his hands in his pockets. He tucked his chin to his chest and tried to make himself as small as possible.

It was an uphill battle.

Bear didn't rush to Waller's doorstep. He took his time, acting like he was going for a nice stroll in the middle of the day. He made sure to wave at everyone who looked his way. More times than not, they smiled and waved back. Even Chicago suburbs were full of people who took good manners at face value. If only they knew what he was capable of.

His ten-minute walk landed him at the end of Waller's driveway. He looked left and right, making sure no nosy neighbors were peering out their windows at him, and walked right up to the front door. That's where he noticed the first red flag.

The door was ajar a few inches. It wouldn't be visible from the road. Anyone passing by on the sidewalk would never have known anything was wrong. But Bear did. And it wasn't just the door. When he pushed forward, he noticed the second red flag.

A smear of blood leading from the threshold, down the hallway, and around the corner, to the living room.

10

BEAR REACHED FOR HIS GUN. HE TOED THE DOOR PARTIALLY SHUT behind him, careful to keep it open enough to make for a quick exit without alerting the neighbors to any suspicious activity. As he inched his way down the hallway, he tried to tune into every single sound inside the house. He heard appliances humming and soft music playing upstairs.

When he reached the corner, Bear poked his head out and followed the trail of blood to a body slumped against the wall. The man was thin, with his head tipped forward and his hands limply sitting in his lap. Bear walked up to him and used the tip of his sidearm to look into the man's face.

It was Waller.

Bear cursed under his breath. What had Mateo or Waller done that would've led to his death? This guy was a genius, the person Mateo had been relying on to build all his green technology for him. If he was dead now, there had to have been a damn good reason. Was this Hughes, or was it someone who had gotten a little trigger happy?

Bear knelt and looked at the wounds in Waller's chest and gut. They weren't bullet holes. His best guess was that they'd surprised him at the front door, gutted him with a couple knives, and then dragged him to this position while he bled out. Maybe they'd interrogated him while he still had some life in him. Or maybe he'd died within a matter of minutes. Some people couldn't handle the shock of knowing they were about to die.

The creak of a floorboard above him alerted Bear to the fact that he wasn't alone. Whoever had killed Waller was still in the house. They could be searching for more information. Or maybe they were just trying to figure out how to hide the body. Either way, Bear wanted to know who had carried out the deed. They'd killed his one good connection to Mateo.

The knife wound told Bear these guys were trying to keep a low profile. They hadn't wanted to attract the attention of the neighbors by firing off a gun, but that didn't mean they weren't armed with something other than the knife they had used to kill Waller. Bear kept his Glock out but decided he'd only use it as a last resort.

Waller's house was smaller than Bear had been expecting. It was built up rather than out. This probably wasn't Waller's main house. Maybe it's where he came to get some work done. Or maybe it's where he came to avoid the real world and throw parties that lasted for days on end. Didn't matter now.

Bear crept up the first set of stairs, keeping to the outside where the steps were likely less noisy. The music got louder, and he started to pick up on a couple of voices. He couldn't make out the words, but they both seemed calm enough. They had no idea there was another person in the house.

As Bear placed his foot on the final step, there was a small *pop* of the wood. The voices cut off. Bear only had a few seconds to launch himself across the hall and into the first open room he could find, hoping no one was inside. It looked like a spare bedroom, full of boxes and plastic tubs. A quick scan told him no one was hiding in there.

A voice floated out from the hallway. "I definitely heard something, man."

"Think it was Waller?"

"No, you idiot. Did you lock the door?"

"Uh, well, I—"

The first man groaned.

"I had my hands full?"

"Someone else could be in here."

The two men were standing at the top of the stairs now, their backs to him. He peeked around the corner and was happy to see the only weapons they had out were a pair of knives. Both looked considerably smaller than him. Whoever they were, they were built for stealth rather than strength.

Good thing Bear had both in spades.

He was standing right behind them by the time the first guy felt his presence. When he turned around, Bear brought a knee to his groin and sent the man to his knees. When the second guy turned around, Bear relieved him of his knife by grabbing his arm and twisting it until the man dropped it. Then Bear sent him sprawling down the stairs.

Bear turned to the first man just in time to jump out of the way of his knife. The blade was serrated. It would've shredded his skin and left huge blotches of blood on the carpet. That wouldn't do. Bear needed to get out of the house without being detected if he had any hope of staying off Hughes' radar.

So, instead, Bear held up his gun and pointed it directly at the man's face. His opponent halted, his eyes going wide. He looked from Bear's gun to the staircase, as if judging whether he was faster than a bullet.

"I wouldn't try it," Bear said.

"Who are you?" the man asked.

"A concerned citizen," Bear said. "Who are you?"

The man shook his head. He looked terrified. So much for being a hardened criminal. Did these two really kill Waller, or had they just shown up to take advantage of the situation? Bear decided to find out.

"You do that downstairs?" he asked.

The man nodded.

"Why?"

"Orders," the man said, like that explained everything.

And maybe it did. Bear looked more closely at the man in front of him. His stance told Bear he was a soldier at some point in his life. The hunting knife could've been from anywhere, but something about the man's simple dress told him otherwise. Bear thought he caught a glance of a necklace around his opponent's neck. Dog tags?

But the track marks up and down his arm put the final piece of the puzzle into place. Hughes was hiring former soldiers to do his dirty work. He was choosing those he could control, if not ones that he could rely on. Did he pay them with money, or did he just hand them the drugs outright?

Bear saw him take a step forward, and Bear matched the movement. "You don't have to do this."

Several emotions passed over the man's face. Fear. Pain. Anger. Determination. When it landed on the last one, Bear knew what to expect. One minute, the man was standing there, and the next he was charging at Bear, brandishing his knife.

Bear didn't shoot him. He stepped to the side and used his gun to block the attack, knocking the knife from his opponent's hand. While the man stumbled and scrambled for his weapon, Bear wrapped one of his arms around his neck and squeezed. The man struggled for a moment before going limp.

Bear had a decision to make. Did he kill him and his buddy? They had murdered a civilian. They'd also attacked Bear. It was well within his right to end their lives. Self-defense. Good citizenry. And one more way to get back at Hughes from a distance.

Why was he hesitating?

He looked back down at the man in his grasp. He saw the marks on his arms and knew what he was going through. Some people don't adjust back to civilian life. It's not like Bear had done a good job living a nine-to-five life.

Bear let the man drop to the floor. He'd be awake again in less than a minute. Bear dragged him to the bedroom and ripped the sheet off the bed, tying it around the man's hands, then around his chest, securing him to the bedframe.

If nothing else, keeping these men alive and putting them in custody would be a bigger thorn in Hughes' side. Bear doubted either of these guys knew where their orders had really come from, but maybe they'd talk enough to leave a paper trail. It was worth the effort.

Bear leaned over the railing and looked for the second man. He'd landed next to Waller's body, smacking his head against the wall and breaking one of his legs. He wasn't going anywhere fast, so Bear elected to leave him for now.

He had more pressing matters.

11

BEAR WASN'T IN A RUSH. THE FIRST MAN WASN'T GOING TO GET OUT of his bonds, the second man still hadn't come around, and no one knew Waller was dead. Bear basically had the run of the house until he called the cops and told them something was wrong.

He was methodical in his search. This was the first major connection to Mateo, and Bear didn't want to miss a single piece of information. If he was lucky, he'd find something that would link both of these men back to Hughes. Bear didn't have high hopes, but it was worth checking, regardless.

He started from the bottom and worked his way up. The basement was where Waller seemed to hold most of his parties. It was full of liquor and craft beer, drugs, and trophies of all his accomplishments.

The first floor was basic. There was little food in the fridge. The cupboards were basically empty. The washer and dryer weren't even hooked up. It confirmed Bear's theory that Waller didn't live here. The boxes upstairs told him that Waller had either recently moved some stuff in—perhaps after beginning his work for Hughes—or he'd never unpacked after he bought the house.

The second floor was initially much more promising. It held three bedrooms, a couple bathrooms, and a few spare rooms. Bear started to look through the boxes in the room he'd hidden in but gave up after ten minutes or so. It was all junk. Literally. There were various parts and pieces that Bear couldn't identify but which were probably like an infinite playground for someone like Waller.

Bear checked the room where he'd tied up the first guy. He was awake now and struggling against his bonds.

"Don't bother," Bear said. "You're not getting out of this one. It's for your own good."

"Please," the man begged. "They're going to kill me."

"The cops will pick you up before that. You'll be safe with them."

The man laughed, but there was a hint of hysteria to it. "You really have no idea what's going on here, do you?"

"Probably not." Bear wasn't even looking at him at this point. He was methodically going through the drawers in Waller's dresser. "Want to fill me in?"

"Please," the man said again. "Please, just let me go."

But Bear had already made up his mind. "Can't do that."

He left the room, leaving the man's begging and screaming behind him, and walked up the last flight of stairs to the top floor.

Jackpot.

This was clearly where Waller had done all of his work. The walls had been knocked out to make one large, open space. It had been filled with lab tables and equipment. Office chairs peppered the area. Even at a glance, Bear could tell there were different sections for different projects. In one area, it looked like Waller had been building a robot. In another, he was fiddling with a solar panel.

The lab was haphazard at best, but if Waller was like any other scientist Bear had ever met, it meant everything was in its place. Organized chaos. That was good news for Bear. It meant he'd find what he was looking for if he nailed down the right spot.

But what *was* he looking for?

Bear entered the area and started opening drawers and sifting through papers. He didn't know exactly, but he'd know it when he found it. He wanted to get an idea of what Waller was working on for Hughes. If he could tie Waller to Mateo and then Mateo to Hughes, they'd have enough of a paper trail to work with.

Bear moved from one table to the next until he was at the far end of the room. Something felt different here. The table was further away from all the others, and there was more safety equipment out. Goggles. Gloves. A fire extinguisher. There was even a burn mark on the wall. Waller had been working on something dangerous.

All the desk drawers were locked, but like the good scatterbrained scientist he was, Waller had left the keys dangling from one of the keyholes. Bear twisted the key in the lock and pulled the drawer open slowly. He half expected to hear ticking.

Instead, he found a stack of papers full of diagrams and scribbled notes. Bear pulled them out and set them on the desk. A lot of it went over his head, but a few keywords jumped out at him.

Easy assembly. Metal-free. Blast radius. Remote trigger mechanism.

Bear took a minute to take it all in. From what he could gather, Waller had been working on a bomb that could pass through metal detectors. It would come in separate parts so as not to raise suspicion. Then, the bomber would just put the pieces together like a puzzle, place it and remotely trigger the device.

Technology like this had existed before Waller, but Bear had never seen anything so small and powerful. He had figured out how to create an incredible amount of devastation with something that could fit in your pocket and was nearly undetectable.

Bear no longer felt bad that Waller had died. Maybe he wasn't as innocent as he had initially thought. Was Waller being pressured to create this device, or had he come up with the design himself? Was he a willing volunteer?

There was no way of finding out now, but it wasn't the most pressing question in Bear's mind. He had seen a couple of notes where Waller had planned on asking Mateo for his opinion, particularly with regard to the price of production. How many would they need, and was there a way to cut costs so they could make more?

Bear was disgusted.

Creating this kind of technology was bad enough, but hiding it behind green technology and the premise of helping the environment was low. Bear wouldn't have been surprised if they had manipulated grants from the government to fund this research.

But this was the kind of connection Bear had been looking for. He knew Waller was working on a new kind of explosive device. He also knew Mateo was or would eventually become aware of it. Now, Bear just had to get in touch with Mateo and convince him to give up Hughes.

For the first time since he'd talked to Jack, Bear felt like they had a chance to get ahead of this.

Bear finished clearing the room, but the other tables only held bits and pieces of projects. It was obvious Waller had abandoned his other pursuits in order to make the bomb his priority, but whether that was voluntary was still a mystery.

As Bear headed toward the staircase, he took one last look at the room behind him. There was a lot more to search through here, and it was likely that he'd never have access to it after he called the authorities, but he was happy with what he had found so far. Besides, he didn't know if Waller was expecting company. He probably had associates. If someone were to come around to check up on him, Bear didn't want to be here.

A glint of something caught his eye under one of the desks. When he walked closer, he noticed that it was a cellphone, probably knocked to the floor and unknowingly kicked into the shadows when Waller was running around making explosive devices.

Bear grabbed the phone and flipped it open. It was a burner like his, only Waller didn't seem to get the concept. It was full of names and numbers. The recent call list hadn't been deleted. The numbers went back as far as a month ago.

Waller could've afforded a better phone, so why did he have this one? Did someone give it to him, or had he purchased it to avoid watchful eyes?

Any interest in answering that question flew out the window when Bear noticed the most recent number that had called Waller. Out of everyone he expected, the name Cara Bishop was the last one he would've guessed.

Cara hadn't included Waller's name in any of her notes. He assumed she had no reason to believe Waller had been involved, but in hindsight, any good journalist would've made note of a dead end. She was obviously keeping information from Bear.

But why?

That was a question for a different day. For now, Bear had more pressing matters. There was one number that occurred more than any of the others, and it belonged to none other than Thomas Mateo. Bear finally had a direct line to their number one lead.

Bear hit the number and waited. It only rang once before Mateo picked up.

"Mitch?" Mateo sounded halfway between worried and annoyed. "Where have you been? I've left you, like, a dozen messages."

Bear stayed silent.

"Mitch? Are you there? We need to talk. I'm afraid something bad is about to happen."

That was Bear's cue. "Something bad has already happened, Mateo."

"What? Who's this? Where's Mitch. If you've hurt him—"

"Sorry to say Mitch now belongs to the dearly departed. The people who did it will be held accountable. For now, that should be the least of your worries."

Mateo's voice was much smaller now. "W-who are you?"

"You've done something really fucking stupid," Bear said. "And I'm the asshole who can get you out of it."

12

SETTING THE MEETING UP WITH MATEO WAS EASIER THAN BEAR HAD expected. Just from their brief conversation over the phone, Bear could tell the other man was in way over his head. His childhood friend was dead, and it'd be next to impossible to deliver on his promises without him.

He was in deep shit.

Bear told him he could help. Said he had the blueprints for the device. He'd exchange them for information on who he was working for. Mateo agreed, but only if he picked the location and they arrived alone. A simple exchange, Mateo had said, with no theatrics. No backup. No bullshit.

Bear agreed.

He wasn't too concerned about Mateo. From the research Bear had conducted, Mateo seemed harmless. He liked earning money and he liked spending it. Most of the controversy he'd been wrapped up in was tied to Waller and his friend's party antics. Usually Mateo was criticized for thinking too big. His visions weren't exactly realistic.

Bear still wondered why Mateo would've agreed to work with someone like Hughes. Was it really just about the money? Mateo had plenty of it, as far as Bear could tell, which meant there had to be something more. He'd make it a point of asking the man when they met.

But while Bear wasn't too concerned about Mateo, he was concerned about what Mateo's money could buy. Would he have hired thugs with him? Was Bear walking into a trap? Would Mateo tip off Hughes in order to gain favor following Waller's death?

Bear doubted it. The man sounded shaken up. He wasn't a hardened criminal. He had cared about Waller, and now his best friend was dead. Whatever was going on here, it sounded like Mateo was having a harder and harder time believing it was all worth it. That would be Bear's opening.

They had agreed to meet in Chicago the following day. Waller had a warehouse outside the city. It was discreet, and only a handful of people knew the location. Mateo was one of them, and after a couple quick directions, Bear was added to that list.

After he hung up with Mateo, Bear called the cops and left the two henchmen to their own devices. The one in the bedroom would live—for now—but the one Bear had kicked down the stairs had suffered head trauma. He might not make it.

Bear had a hard time caring.

He left the house, checking to make sure he didn't have any blood on his clothes, and caught up to his cabdriver, who had made it a considerable way through his book by the time Bear returned.

"All good?" the man asked.

"Yeah," Bear said. "Just had to pick something up from a friend of mine."

"Good deal," the man said, driving away from the curb.

About five minutes out, they passed two police cruisers with their sirens blaring. They were headed toward Waller's house at top-speed.

"Looks like they've got somewhere important to be," the cabbie said.

"Yeah." Bear didn't take his eyes off the scenery passing them by. "Hope everyone is okay."

He tuned out the cabbie's reply, choosing to let the drive lull him into a trance.

When they made it back to the city, Bear found the cheapest hotel room cash could buy and kept a low profile. After a bite to eat and a hot shower, he crashed for the night, falling asleep to the news. They were still running the story about the bombing in Germany, saying authorities had a suspect but that no information was to be released at the time so as not to hinder the investigation.

Bear chuckled. Even if they were trying to haul Jack in, they'd never find him. It was a dead end.

BEAR WOKE up refreshed the next morning. He grabbed coffee on his way out, knowing full well it was going to be some of the worst he'd ever had. He didn't care. He just wanted the most amount of caffeine in his system in the shortest amount of time. He didn't even taste it on its way down.

Mateo had wanted to meet by nine in the morning. Apparently, he had plenty of other things to do in the city and didn't want this to put him behind schedule. Bear had almost asked him what he valued more, his life or his precious schedule, but he'd decided to hold his tongue. The guy was already freaked out. Better to not make it worse.

But it was good to know Mateo's work ethic wasn't slowed down by a little thing like murder.

Bear took the train out of the city and decided to walk the

couple miles it would take to get to the warehouse. It was in an industrial part of town, and he wanted to get a lay of the land in case this whole thing went sideways.

All things considered, however, Bear was feeling pretty good about the meeting. It didn't sound like it would be hard to convince Mateo to switch sides, and if he could get the eccentric billionaire to point the finger at Hughes, then the Director of National Intelligence's entire plan went up in smoke.

But that was also the exact reason why Bear was being so cautious. If he was feeling this at ease about the meeting, then something was bound to go wrong. Hughes was too smart to let Mateo out of his sights for long. The window they had was narrow, and if Bear had to run protection on Mateo until they got him somewhere safe, it was going to take a lot more resources than he currently had at his fingertips.

It took some effort, but Bear forced himself to be more aware, more vigilant. There was no point in going into this thinking he was ahead of the curve. That kind of mentality always had a way of biting him in the ass in the end.

So, Bear stood by and waited. He kept his eye on the warehouse entrance. He waited for his watch to tick closer to nine. The morning was quiet. There was a touch of fog in the distance. It was cooler than it had been over the last few days. Bear decided to make his move.

Why was it that his instincts were always right when he least wanted them to be?

13

Mateo had given him the code to the warehouse. A little number pad next to the door unlocked it soundlessly, and Bear pulled it open, greeted by a burst of stale, dusty air. Mateo had mentioned that this particular warehouse wasn't used as often anymore. Bear had to agree. It smelled like it had been part of the Industrial Revolution.

Bear let the door click shut behind him, and immediately all the hair on the back of his neck stood on end. It could've been because he suddenly felt trapped. He resisted the urge to test if the door would open back up behind him. It also could've been that he didn't know the layout of the building—the rooms, the levels, the exits. He also resisted the urge to grab his gun for reassurance.

Once Bear made it through the entrance, which was just a simple hallway, the building opened up in front of him. The warehouse was completely open from top to bottom. Skylights three stories up lit the entire building, shining light into almost every corner. He was thankful the sun was out today.

Along the walls were stairs and catwalks leading to side rooms.

Mateo had told him his office was on the third floor, right-hand side. He'd be waiting inside, and they'd have half an hour to come to some sort of agreement.

Mateo had conducted the phone call like he was setting up a business meeting, not like he was meeting the one person in the world who could possibly get him out of the mess he'd created.

Bear stood in full view of the entire building for a solid minute. He took it all in, searching every corner for movement. He kept his ears open, but only heard the wind whipping through an open door somewhere. If Mateo was here, he wasn't making any sound.

Even though he would've liked to clear the entire building before he holed himself up in a room with a man he barely knew, Bear moved to the right side of the building and began climbing the stairs. Again, he resisted pulling out his Glock. The hairs on the back of his neck were relentless, and he felt a pit forming in his stomach. Maybe his initial conclusion that this was far too easy was right on the money.

There was no purpose to having offices with windows in a place where your view included four steel walls and a bunch of shipping containers. But that didn't make Bear wish any less that he'd be able to look into Mateo's office before opening the door into the unknown.

But there was no point in delaying the inevitable.

Bear threw caution to the wind, grabbed the doorknob to Mateo's office, and flung the door open. He braced himself to react, either by grabbing his gun or diving out of the way if the scene that greeted him was less than favorable.

What he wasn't expecting was Cara Bishop.

What's more, he definitely wasn't expecting to see her standing over a dying Thomas Mateo with a bloody hunting knife in her hand.

Bear blinked once, twice, three times, and then grabbed his

gun from his waist, and kept it pointed to the ground. He looked from Cara's pale and shocked face to Mateo's bloody chest. He was gasping his last breath just as Bear entered the room.

Cara was covered in blood. It was all over her hands, either where she had plunged the knife into his chest or where she had pulled it out. The knees of her pale pink pants were also bloody. Had she knelt by his side while he died?

"I-I found h-him like this," Cara said, turning to Bear. There were tears streaming down her face. "I-I just w-walked in a-and found him."

Bear opened his mouth to respond when he heard a door slam somewhere in the building. He cocked his head and listened to the echo. It sounded like it came from the back of the building.

Bear walked up to Cara cautiously and pulled the knife from her hands. He wiped it down and tossed it to the side. He cast a single glance at Mateo, but his blank eyes and still body told Bear that it was too late for him.

Instead, Bear grabbed Cara by the hand and dragged her out of the office behind him. He kept his ears open for any more sounds, but the warehouse was dead silent. Even the whistling wind from earlier had quieted down.

Bear led Cara down the stairs quickly and quietly. He kept his hand around hers, and he couldn't help but notice how much she was shaking. His anger that she hadn't listened to him was abated by his instinct to make sure she was okay.

When they reached the bottom of the stairs, Bear took in her complexion. She was still pale, but there was a flush to her cheeks that made him think she wouldn't pass out on him. Her eyes were wild, and she still had a death grip on his hand.

"I need you to hide while I try to find whoever did this," he said.

"What?" Cara's voice was shrill. "No. You can't leave me."

"It'll only be for a minute. I just need to make sure we're alone."

"No, please," she begged. "Please, you can't leave me. Please."

"Okay, okay, okay." Bear held back a groan. Having her in tow would complicate matters. "Stay right behind me, okay? In my shadow at all times."

Cara nodded vigorously.

"And I'm going to need my hand back."

Cara looked down at their interlinked hands and let go. She immediately latched onto his elbow. Not ideal, but something he could work with.

Bear turned toward the back of the building and made his way along the outer wall. Every step closer to the back door made Bear feel more and more sure they'd missed their opportunity. When he reached the back entrance and tried to open it, finding it locked, he knew he was right.

He cursed under his breath.

"What's wrong?" Cara whispered.

"Whoever did this kept the back door propped. It locked when they escaped. They'll be in the wind now."

"What about us?" Cara asked. "Are we locked in here?"

"Let's find out."

Bear led her back the way they had come and found the front door still opened. The wind whipped as they made their way across the street to an empty storefront down the road. No one else was in sight. Whoever had killed Mateo was either long gone or watching them from the shadows. Bear stayed vigilant.

The storefront wasn't locked. The fact that it wasn't covered in dust and a few bookshelves had been moved to form a little barrier against the wind told Bear that the homeless had probably taken up residence here recently. They'd likely moved closer to the city once the weather had turned. It'd be a little warmer there, plus their chances to make a little money were higher.

Bear maneuvered Cara to a plastic chair sitting in the corner. He found a large scrap of a sheet and began wiping the blood off her hands. The fabric wasn't exactly clean, but it was better than leaving her the way she was.. Mostly, the sheet just smeared the blood around and turned her hands pink.

She was still shivering, and Bear noticed her eyes had that distant look he'd seen more often than he cared to admit. Some people just couldn't handle tragedy. He couldn't blame her. Something like this hadn't been in the job description.

Bear took off his jacket and draped it around her shoulders. He knelt in front of her and waited until her gaze focused in on him. Once he knew she was paying attention to him, he only had one thing to say.

"Tell me everything."

14

"I-I don't know," she stammered. "I was just there and then he was just dead."

Bear shook her shoulders gently. "Listen to me, I can only help you if you tell me exactly what happened. Every detail. Everything you remember. You're a journalist, right? This is your job. This is what you're good at. You told me yourself. Give me the facts."

Cara took a deep breath and Bear saw something shift inside of her. She was going into investigative mode. Her voice was still quiet, but it was steady. The shivering had almost stopped.

"I found out Mateo was meeting with someone this morning. My source suggested I arrive early and hide close by. Record the whole thing."

"Who's your source?"

Cara shook her head and kept her mouth clamped shut.

Bear stood up and paced the length of the room. He fought to keep his voice level. "I need to know everything. *Everything.* Your prints could be all over that place. Do you understand how much trouble you're in? You have no idea how big this goes."

Cara stood up and matched Bear in anger, if not in height. "I do know how big this goes. I know about Hughes, remember? All the way to the White House, that's how far. In more ways than one."

"What do you mean in more ways than one?"

Cara waved away the comment. "This isn't the time for that. I can't tell you who my source is. It's a deal breaker. Full stop."

Bear considered, for the first time, that Cara's source might be bigger than he initially thought. Could her source be in the White House? A staffer? An old friend or former flame? Someone bigger who had gotten wind of Hughes' plan and wanted to do the right thing without exposing themselves?

But Cara wasn't going to budge, and something told Bear that no amount of force or coercion was going to change that. But there was still a growl in his voice when he spoke. "Keep talking."

Cara sat back down and pulled Bear's jacket tighter around her shoulders. "I knew the code, so I snuck in. Found Mateo's office and hid in the next room. I had everything set up. I'd be able to hear their whole conversation and they wouldn't even know I was there."

Bear kept his mouth shut. It was a stupid, reckless thing to do. Before talking to Mateo, he would've checked the surrounding rooms to make sure they were alone. He would've looked for recording devices.

But interrupting her again wouldn't do him any favors.

"Mateo was there for only a minute or two before someone walked in. He seemed surprised."

"Did he say who the other person was?" Bear asked.

Cara leveled him with a look. "Don't you think that would've been the first thing I said?"

"Fair enough."

"Mateo seemed surprised. Asked what the other guy was doing

there. Asked what was going on. The other guy said, 'Fixing your mistakes.' His voice was deep, steady. He didn't sound angry. More like he was resigned."

A shiver passed through Cara as she recalled the events. Tears started gathering in her eyes, but she wiped them away and kept talking.

"There was movement and Mateo groaned. He sounded surprised again. He tried to say something, but couldn't. I heard him fall to the ground. I stayed as quiet as I could. I just kept praying that the other guy didn't hear me. Didn't see me. Even when I heard him leave the room, I was too scared to go see what happened."

Bear knelt in front of Cara. "What'd you do next?"

"Counted to sixty in my head. Three times. I heard Mateo groaning. I knew what I was going to find, but you just...can't prepare for something like that. When I eventually went out there, I saw blood everywhere. Mateo was covered in it. His hands, his chest. It was all over the floor. And he was trying to pull the knife out of his chest."

Her eyes were distant again. Recalling the events was like muscle memory now. She wasn't reliving it anymore. She was stating the facts. Still, a tear dropped down her cheek and disappeared into one of the folds of Bear's jacket.

"He was panicked. I just wanted to help. I don't know why I did it. I know you're not supposed to. I knew my prints would be on it. But I couldn't just leave him like that. He was so scared."

Bear decided to help her along. "So you pulled the knife out."

Cara nodded. "He was trying to say something, but I couldn't hear him. It was like he didn't have enough air in his lungs to speak. And then thirty seconds later, you came in."

Bear stood again. Her story made sense. Maybe if they hadn't heard someone else leave the building, he would've questioned it a little more. As it was, Cara seemed totally innocent in this situation. Not that the authorities would see it that way.

As if on cue, Bear's ears perked up at the sound of sirens in the distance. "We've gotta move."

"We shouldn't have left the scene," Cara said. "It's going to look suspicious."

"It already looks suspicious," Bear replied. "Trust me, the cops aren't our friends right now."

"Trust you?" Cara said. "I don't even know you."

"And yet you seemed so surprised when I wasn't willing to risk everything to trust you yesterday. I guess we finally understand each other."

"Doubtful."

Bear sighed. Fighting wasn't going to get them anywhere. "You know how high this goes. You don't think the cops are in on it? At least some of them? If they find you covered in blood at the crime scene, they'll charge you with murder before you can even ask for a lawyer. Mateo was a public figure. This is a high-profile case. They'll want to close it quickly."

When Cara didn't argue, he assumed she agreed with him.

"Is your car nearby?" Bear asked.

She nodded. "It's two streets over."

"Then let's go."

Bear left their hideout with Cara on his heels. The sirens were coming in quick, and the two of them wasted no time running to her car. Bear held out his hand for the keys and she handed them over wordlessly. He checked for tracking devices and found none. When he figured it was safe, they piled into the car and sped off toward the city.

The journey was silent. Cara kept pulling the coat tighter around her shoulders. Bear cranked up the heat in the car. She stared at her bloody hands. He stared at the road ahead.

Cara was first to break the silence. They were driving along a side street filled with businesses. It was mostly bars and restaurants, but a few retailers dotted the sidewalk. Bear stopped at a red light and scanned the area. He checked the rearview mirror. His side mirrors. He cranked his head to the left. Cara spoke from the right.

"Bear?"

Bear twisted his head toward her. He followed her gaze to the shop sitting outside the passenger window. They sold electronics. Their shop window was full of TVs that played the news. Bear and Cara's faces plastered the airwaves. Wanted for murder. Extremely dangerous.

Cara choked on a sob. "Oh, God."

Bear was still trying to process it. How did that happen so fast? It had been, what, twenty minutes? That meant this had been the plan all along. If the hit went off successfully, Mateo's murderer would call it in and they'd run the story on the news.

A car honked. Bear's gaze snapped to the vehicle behind him. A man threw up his arms and gestured toward the light. Bear looked forward. It was green. He put his foot to the gas pedal and eased forward, gaining momentum slowly and steadily.

"We need to lay low," Bear said. "We need to get somewhere safe."

Cara didn't say anything. He was beginning to take her silence as approval.

Bear pressed down on the gas pedal a little harder.

15

BEAR DIDN'T HAVE A SAFEHOUSE IN CHICAGO. THEY'D HAVE TO RELY on a seedy hotel. He didn't bother going back to the one he was in last night. Better not to double dip when you're fugitives from the law.

Sometimes Bear couldn't help but be amazed at how many times he'd been on the run. They said it took ten thousand hours to master something. Bear wondered how close he was to that number.

They dumped the car on the outskirts of the city and hopped on the train. Bear's coat was long enough that it covered Cara's bloody hands and knees. They got a few strange looks, but this was Chicago. There were a bunch of weirdos on the train. He and Cara were probably the most normal out of all of them.

When the Red Line hit the Loop, Cara looked over at Bear, as if expecting for him to get up and off the train. He kept his eyes forward. This area would be easier to disappear in, but it would also be harder to catch any tails they might have.

And Bear wanted to know if they were being watched.

Instead, he waited a few more stops and got off at a random platform just outside downtown Chicago. It'd be easier to find a shitty motel out here anyway. Everything in the middle of the city would be high-profile, and that was the last thing they needed right now.

When their feet hit the pavement and Bear headed North, Cara had to jog to catch up. She was silent for only a moment before she asked the inevitable.

"When can we go back to my apartment?"

"We can't."

Her steps faltered and she struggled to catch up to Bear's pace again. "What do you mean we can't? Everything I have is there. Notes, everything."

"It's gone. Just accept it."

Cara grabbed Bear's arm to try to get him to slow down, but it didn't have any affect. "We have to—"

Bear came to an abrupt halt and Cara nearly tripped over her own feet. He turned on her, trying to control his anger, his frustration, his hopelessness about this entire situation.

"They know who we are. The first thing they're going to do is go to your apartment. They're probably already there. Any information you have is gone. All we have is what you decided to write down in the notebook you gave me."

Cara lifted an eyebrow at him. "What do you mean what I *decided* to tell you?"

"Ever heard of a guy named Waller?"

She had the audacity to look sheepish. "Mateo's friend." Her eyes grew wide. "Oh God. We have to tell him. We have to warn him."

"Don't bother." Bear started walking again. "He's already dead."

"What? How?" There was a small pause. "Did you kill him?"

Bear laughed. "No. Someone got to him before I did. But now you're thinking smart. Don't trust anyone."

"Who killed him?"

"No idea," Bear said. "They were just a couple of junkie ex-soldiers. But whoever sent them probably also sent the person who killed Mateo."

"Hughes?"

"Maybe," Bear said. "Or he could have a lackey who does his dirty work for him."

"Plausible deniability."

"Bingo. Another point to Team Bishop." Bear heard Cara open her mouth to retort, but he didn't give her a chance. "What I can't figure out is why you didn't mention him at all."

"A girl's gotta have her secrets."

Bear shot her a look. "Keeping secrets from me is not a good idea. Not if you want to survive this."

"Is that a threat?"

He laughed. "No. I have no interest in killing you, Ms. Bishop. In fact, I've gone to great lengths to keep you alive. And somehow you keep throwing yourself in the line of danger."

"It's part of the job," she said.

"It's stupid."

There was a momentary break in conversation. Bear kept his strides long and his pace unrelenting. Cara was always a step or two behind him, but close enough that if something went wrong, he'd be able to pull her out of harm's way.

"Why didn't you tell me about Waller?" he asked.

"My source told me not to."

"Ah, your infamous source." Any frustration that had left Bear thanks to the brisk walk had flooded right back into him. "Who is that again? I forget."

"Nice try."

"Your number was in his phone," Bear said. "Waller's, I mean. Rookie move. If someone else had found his cell, they'd be able to trace it right back to you."

"Guess it doesn't really matter now," Cara said, a hint of despondency in her voice. "My face is all over the news."

Bear bit his tongue to keep him from telling her that she wouldn't be in this situation if she had just listened to him in the first place. But there was no point in beating a dead horse, no matter how good it made him feel.

The rest of the walk was continued in silence. Bear lost track of how long they had been walking. His brain was only capable of two things: keeping an eye on their surroundings and moving constantly forward.

He only allowed himself to slow down once he spotted a cheap motel in the distance. They stuck to the shadows, and Bear watched the parking lot for a few minutes. Not a lot of traffic. It looked like only two of the bedrooms facing the main road were lit up. That didn't mean more weren't occupied, but it certainly boded well that this was a quiet place to hunker down for the night.

Bear looked over at Cara. She was still wearing his jacket, which completely engulfed her small frame. It hung low enough that her bloody knees were barely visible. Her hands were still slightly pink, but no one would be able to guess it was blood. He was in a better state than she was, but he was also a lot more recognizable.

"You have a hair tie?"

Cara looked up at him with a strange look on her face. "Yeah, why? You want to braid your beard?"

He chuckled humorlessly and pulled a wad of cash out of his pocket. "Tie your hair back, then go in there and get us a room. Two beds."

"Obviously."

He ignored her comment. "And make sure it's near one of the exits."

"How am I supposed to say that without sounding suspicious?"

It was almost cute how bad she was at this. Almost. "We're here *because* no one will be suspicious. You think that's the weirdest thing anyone has ever requested?"

"Fair enough."

Cara took the money and put her hair up in a messy bun. She adjusted the coat so it covered as much of her clothes as possible and then strode out of the shadows, across the parking lot, and through the front door of the motel.

For a brief moment, Bear worried that she might cut and run. But then he remembered that she didn't have anywhere else to go. Besides, she'd be digging her own grave.

Worse comes to worst, he'd be losing sixty bucks and maybe a few minutes of sleep.

16

CARA DID NOT, IN FACT, CHOOSE TO CUT AND RUN. INSTEAD, SHE walked back out of the lobby and waved a pair of keycards in his direction. She at least had the wherewithal to circle the building and go in the back entrance where they wouldn't be seen together. Looked like Ms. Bishop was a quicker study than he gave her credit for.

She had also landed a room right next to the exit. A pair of twin beds, a simple TV, and a small bathroom greeted them when she unlocked the door. The carpet was dark with age and dirt, the wallpaper was peeling, and there was a strange funk in the air.

But it didn't matter. They had a couple of beds and a relatively safe place to sleep for the night.

Bear made a beeline for the TV remote and flipped on the news. He wasn't looking forward to what he would find there, but he knew he had to stay on top of this before it got even more out of control.

For her part, Cara sank down on the edge of her bed and twisted the ends of her hair between her fingers. She stared at the screen with wide eyes, tears gathering in the corners. She was steadier than she had been earlier in the day, but Bear could tell she was still processing the whole situation.

Meanwhile, he was already planning four steps ahead. Getting out of the city would be ideal, but he knew he couldn't go far. Waller and Mateo had died here, which meant there could be something else in Chicago waiting to be uncovered.

Bear wracked his brain for who he could reach out to. So many of his contacts lived in the shadows, and right now his face was plastered all over national television. On the bright side, no one was talking about the bombings in Germany right now. On the other hand, the whole country knew his name and face. Clearing this up was going to be a bitch.

From his right, Bear heard Cara groan. "My career is over."

Bear tried to keep the rage from bursting out of him, but it was too much to keep inside. He stood up so quickly, Cara gasped and scooted across the bed to the far corner. She looked up at him with fear in her eyes, and the only thing he could think was, *Finally, you're scared enough.*

"Your career?" he said. "Our *lives* are over. You get that, right?"

Cara sputtered, but he didn't let her talk. Instead, he pointed at the TV. It took all his self-control not to throw the remote at the screen in the hopes of shattering it and ridding them of the unfortunate circumstances they found themselves in.

"Our lives are over," he repeated. "You get that, right? What the hell was Jack thinking, setting me up with a kid who cares more about her career than her own goddamn life?"

"How dare you," Cara said, regaining her composure. "How dare you even pretend to know anything about me. Do I care about my career? Of course I do! I've spent most of my life building toward this moment. To win awards and recognition? No. *To help people.* What have you done? Huh?"

"A hell of a lot more than you. You're a child begging to sit at the big kid's table. Well, this is what happens. You went and fucked the whole thing up."

"Me?" Cara's voice was shrill now. "I probably saved your life!"

Bear laughed. He couldn't help it. The cackle just burst forth from his chest, uninhibited. "How the hell do you figure?"

"If you had gone in there first, you'd probably be dead. Did that little fact ever occur to you between constantly ridiculing and berating me?"

It had occurred to him, but he wasn't going to give her even a single win. "And what about you, huh? How did you manage to survive? You should've been as dead as Mateo. Why aren't you?"

Cara either didn't have an answer or refused to give the one she did have. Her silence rang throughout the room. Bear waved it off.

"I'm going out. Stay, or leave. I don't care."

Bear didn't bother looking for her reaction. He spun on his heel, wrenched the door open, and slammed it shut behind him. The cool air did little to affect his core temperature, which was burning with the heat of his anger.

Bear struck out in a random direction and walked with his head high, not caring if anyone saw him. It had only been a few hours since Mateo's death, which meant it wasn't even noon. The sun was high and the sky was clear. He'd be an easy target for anyone who recognized his face.

He didn't care.

He found himself hoping someone would start something. At the very least, it would give him a change of clothes. At most, it would let him work off a little steam. This whole situation had gotten away from him and he wasn't sure how he'd be able to get back out from under it.

After about half a mile, Bear's blood pressure started to ease.

His heartbeat slowed. The anger flushed from his system. He was acutely aware of the people who gave him a double-take. It's not like that didn't normally happen, but now there was a chance they might have recognized his face and were trying to figure out where they knew him from.

Bear slipped into an alley and stuck to the shadows. Things were bad enough. He didn't need to get caught doing something stupid like starting a fight in broad daylight. He needed a plan, and he needed one fast.

He knew he could get to Canada and survive in the wilderness for a while. No one would be able to find him, but his life as he knew it would be over. He'd have to find a way to reach out to Jack and get both their names cleared, but with Jack on the run just as much—if not more than—Bear, it was unlikely they'd be able to link up again anytime soon.

Besides, Jack was counting on him. He couldn't drop the ball now, not when they were closer than they'd ever been.

Bear reached for the papers he had grabbed from Waller's home and realized they were in the pocket of the jacket he had let Cara wear. He patted down the back pocket of his jeans and realized he still had her notebook, though it paled in comparison to the designs for the bomb. That was going to be the best way to link what Waller and Mateo had been working on with whatever Hughes had in mind.

Without the blueprint, his investigation was dead in the water. They wouldn't get another opportunity like that, not now that both men were dead.

Bear noticed a beat-up car from his hiding spot in the alley. It would be so easy to steal it and make a getaway. He could disappear off the radar so much easier without Cara Bishop in tow. She'd get pinched sooner rather than later, but what did he care? She'd probably be safer in jail.

Except maybe not. According to the guy Bear had left tied to the bed in Waller's house, the cops were not to be trusted. That wasn't exactly new territory for Bear. But even if Cara managed to stay clear of the authorities, she was right—her career was over. Mateo's throng of ravenous fans would make sure of that.

What would all those conspiracy theorists do if they realized they had been right all along?

Bear was seriously contemplating pushing off from the alley wall and stealing that car when a thought struck him. Mateo had been terrified. Even before Bear had told him that Waller had died, he'd been afraid for his friend's life. He'd been afraid for his own.

He had been getting cold feet.

When Mateo had agreed to meet with Bear, he was getting ready to back out. He had agreed to the meeting because Bear had been his only hope of getting out of a situation of his own making. What if Mateo had already been on a hit list, and his meeting with Bear had been the opportunity they had needed all along?

Either Mateo hadn't wanted to start Word War III or he had gotten wind of the plan's true motive and tried to pull out. One way or another, it led to his death. Hughes had been having private meetings with Mateo for the last year. He would've been privy to the eccentric billionaire's change of heart.

It always came back to Hughes.

If nothing else, Cara Bishop had a source she was willing to do anything to protect. If her informant wasn't someone huge, she would've given up their name a long time ago. For the first time, Bear gave Cara the benefit of the doubt. Maybe she really did know what she was doing.

One way or another, he had to figure out who her source was.

It was time to play ball.

17

BEAR MADE HIS WAY BACK TO THE HOTEL, DOING A MUCH BETTER JOB of keeping his head down. It was mid-afternoon by this time, which meant traffic was starting to pick up. Soon, there'd be people everywhere, and he'd no doubt run into someone who was looking to be a hero.

When he got back to the hotel, Bear did a perimeter check and noted which cars in the parking lot had been there before and which had been swapped out. Nothing seemed out of the ordinary, but he wasn't willing to take any more chances than he already had. They'd stay here for a single night and then move on.

To where, he didn't know.

When Bear inserted the keycard into the door and walked back into the room, he was only mildly surprised that Cara was nowhere to be found. His last words to her weren't exactly kind, and he didn't blame her for not wanting to stick it out with a guy as volatile as he'd been over the last few hours.

He was even less surprised to realize that she had taken his jacket with her. He hadn't told her about the blueprint for the bomb, but she'd find it sooner rather than later and start putting two and two together. What would she do with that information? Probably something reckless.

Bear felt a pinch in his chest. She drove him crazy the way she ran head-first into situations, but he never wanted her to get killed. Maybe roughed up a bit so some sense would be knocked into her. But he never once wished she was dead.

There was no way she'd survive out there without him. She was smart, sure, but she'd take too many risks trying to pin down the rest of the story. One way or another, she'd get caught. What would happen then? Would the police smear her pictures all over the news and come up with some story about how she's a deranged individual? Or would she just disappear under a black hood, never to be heard from again?

Did she have any family? Would anyone miss her?

Bear pulled out the burner phone he had picked up and stared down at it. There were a couple people he could call who'd be able to help track her down, but every single one of their numbers could be traced. It'd take too long to find a way to get through to them without alerting everyone who had their eyes on him.

Right as he was about to ignore all his instincts, the door clicked open and Cara walked in carrying a shopping bag in each hand. Her hair was wet and she looked cleaner than when he had left. Looked like she had taken advantage of the shower while he was away.

She gave him a wry smile, but he caught the relief in her eyes.

"I knew you'd be back."

"And I knew you wouldn't leave." He nodded toward the bag. "What'd you get?"

"A couple sandwiches, a beanie, a new pair of pants, and this." She pulled out shaving cream and a razor.

"What's that for?" he asked.

"It's for you." She laughed. "You need to shave that mess off your face if we're going to get out of town."

Bear instinctively touched a hand to his face. "Not a chance."

Cara rolled her eyes and dumped the contents of the bag on one of the beds. "You're the expert."

Bear grabbed for one of the sandwiches and unwrapped it, eyeing Cara in the process. "You seem different."

"Different how?"

"Chipper."

"Chipper?" Cara laughed again. "I'm barely hanging on by a thread, but I'm glad I'm coming off as *chipper*."

Bear took a bite of his ham sandwich and didn't say anything.

"I got a phone call."

That made Bear pause. "From who?"

"My source." Cara eyed him like she as waiting for him to ask who it was. He didn't. "They wanted to make sure I was okay."

"Did you tell them where we were?"

Cara rolled her eyes. "Of course not."

Bear held up a hand. He didn't want to start another fight. "Just making sure."

"They didn't say much, just that they were going to work on getting our names off the news."

"In exchange for what?"

Cara knit her eyebrows together. "Nothing."

"Nobody does anything for nothing."

"Some people do things for the right reason. He knows we're innocent."

"I guess." Bear couldn't let the slip slide. "So, your source is a *he*?"

Cara flinched but recovered quickly. "That doesn't exactly narrow it down."

"I know." Bear decided to pivot. "I have a plan."

Cara finally unwrapped her sandwich and took a bite. Around a mouthful of turkey, she said, "You do?"

"Part of one at least."

"This ought to be good."

Bear ignored her. "How do you feel about Wisconsin?"

"I am a fan of cheese."

"I have a buddy there who might be able to help us lay low for a minute. It's pretty remote."

"Do you trust him?"

"I do." Bear weighed how much he should give away. "He used to work for the government. Retired maybe ten or fifteen years ago."

"You don't think he's compromised?"

Bear chuckled. "Rodger isn't exactly an easy guy to win over. He's pretty critical of the White House. Has been from the beginning. He saw a lot of action overseas. Doesn't trust a whole lot of people."

"But he trusts you?"

Bear puffed out his chest. "I'm a very trustworthy person."

"I'm beginning to suspect as much." Cara polished off her sandwich and stood up, wiping the crumbs from her lap. "When do we leave?"

Bear walked over to the window and parted the curtains. It was still light out. They needed sleep. He still needed a shower. It was a risk not getting out of the city immediately, but they wouldn't be able to do much without the cover of darkness anyway.

"Early in the morning, before sunrise." Bear ignored Cara's groan. "I need to set a few things up and we need to recharge. Then we're off."

"Cruel and unusual punishment."

"You've survived this much."

"This might be the thing that breaks me."

Bear laughed, but he couldn't help questioning the shift in Cara's mood. She was at ease now—such a stark difference from when he last left her. Was it relief that he had returned? Comfort in knowing her source was going to do anything he could to help them avoid detection? Or was something else going on?

He didn't like not knowing, and he knew his contact in Wisconsin wouldn't like it much either.

But what other choice did he have?

18

―――――

"THERE ARE A FEW THINGS YOU HAVE TO UNDERSTAND ABOUT Rodger Goldstone."

Cara rolled her head to look at Bear, her eyes half open and still crusty with sleep. "Did he make his fortune in cheese?"

"He did not." Bear kept driving, his eyes on the road. "But he does keep a few cows as company."

Cara groaned. "Don't tell me we're laying low on a farm."

"It's a good place to hide out."

Cara covered her head with Bear's jacket.

Bear smiled. He had woken her up around three in the morning, having only gotten a couple hours of sleep himself. He had been keeping one eye on the television and one eye on coordinating their escape from the city. In the end, he and Rodger had determined that the best course of action was the simplest.

So, Bear had roused Cara around three and they'd quietly exited the hotel, heading toward a side road with numerous parked cars. As luck would have it, a 1991 Toyota Camry with a dent in the passenger side bumper sat on the corner just waiting to be jacked.

"We're stealing cars now?" Cara had asked.

"Borrowing."

"Are you planning on returning it?"

"I'm not planning to keep it," Bear said.

She had rolled her eyes but didn't argue. It looked like Cara's journalistic integrity only went so far. Then again, they were on the run as fugitives wanted for murder. A little grand theft auto on the side didn't seem like such a big deal in comparison.

Bear had taken a metal coat hanger from the hotel. He untwisted it and popped the lock on the car within seconds. Cara piled in without complaint and they got on the road. The plan was to meet Rodger halfway to his place, dump this car, walk to a meeting point, and join him in his. There was still a chance they were being watched and any amount of maneuvering wouldn't stop that, but it was the best idea they had. And Rodger was willing to take the risk.

"So, what are the few things I have to understand about Rodger Goldstone?" Cara asked, unburying her head from his jacket. "And keep it to the bullet points."

"Rodger is a highly-decorated soldier who has seen more combat than almost anyone I know. He turned in his gun for a desk when his daughter got pregnant. He wasn't around much as a father, and he didn't want to make the same mistake with his grandkids."

Cara sat up but didn't say anything. Bear could tell he'd already hooked her on Rodger.

"The man would do anything for his family – and he has. He spent twenty years behind a desk working in the Pentagon. He knows things that would curdle *my* blood. He has a lot of secrets stored in that big head of his. It's no wonder he's paranoid."

"If he's got so many secrets, how'd he get out?"

Bear laughed. "He worked for the government, not a gang."

"Is there a difference?"

"More rules," Bear offered. "But fair point."

"Seriously, though, I'm surprised. You'd think they'd still want him on board."

"They do. And he does sometimes offer his expertise as a consultant. But only as an independent contractor. He said he'll never work for the government again. Not like he used to."

"Makes you wonder why," Cara said.

"Not me. I feel better off not knowing."

"So, what's he do now?"

"He takes care of his farm. Takes care of his family. Every couple of months, he flies to D.C. Says it's better that he can keep an eye on everyone this way."

"How did you two meet?"

Bear let the question hang in the air for a moment. It was a complicated, messy story. Jack had been involved, as usual. There'd been a shootout. Someone they had all cared about had died. He wasn't sure Cara needed to know the details. And he wasn't sure he wanted to share them.

Bear flicked the turn signal and made a right onto a side street. "We met overseas during a joint task force operation. Jack and I thought we were hot shit back then. Didn't like following orders. We were so stupid. Major General Goldstone proved pretty quickly he wasn't going to stand for that. Only took him a week to break us."

"A week sounds like a long time."

Bear laughed. "Something tells me he had the time and energy to go a lot longer than that."

"And now you're friends?"

Bear shrugged. "We respect each other. We're willing to stick our necks out for each other."

"Sounds like a friend to me."

"Maybe." It was hard to describe the relationship you had with a former commanding officer. That respect and deference never went away. It was hard to call that person a friend. The word didn't sound like enough. The trust went deeper than that.

"But you said he's paranoid?"

Bear took a left turn and checked his rearview mirror. So far, he hadn't spotted anyone following them. "He's vigilant."

"That's just a nice way of saying paranoid."

"He has his reasons. The man is 79 years old and could still kick my ass six ways from Sunday. He's seen everything. Done everything. He's killed the things that go bump in the night. If he's worried, he's got good reason to be."

"Sounds like you respect him."

"I'd be stupid not to."

Silence filled the car after that. Bear didn't feel like he had done Rodger Goldstone justice, but sometimes it was just better to meet the man in person. And soon enough, they would. He'd be lying if he wasn't curious how Goldstone and Ms. Bishop would mix. As Bear had quickly learned, Cara had a stubborn streak that was hard to beat out. Depending on his mood, Goldstone might not stand for that.

Or maybe he'd encourage it. Like he had done with Jack and Bear.

Bear kept driving North. After about ten minutes, he heard Cara snoring softly. He would've preferred getting more sleep, but the importance of keeping to the cover of the night was paramount. They needed to move undetected. They needed to ensure they didn't bring anyone to Rodger's doorstep.

As the sun started to peek out over the horizon, Bear's craving for coffee intensified. There was something about a crisp November morning and the breaking of dawn that made you want to inject hot java directly into your veins. But there was no chance he was going to take that risk this morning.

By now, most televisions around the country would've shown their pictures. A lot of people still wouldn't be able to pick Bear and Cara out of a lineup, but the chances were higher now than they were last night. He didn't want to raise any flags now that they had successfully made it out of Chicago.

Bear half-expected patrol cars to be out in droves, especially overnight when the cops knew he'd be more likely to run. Maybe they just didn't want to cause a panic by locking up the city. More than likely, Hughes and his goonies just wanted to see where Bear was heading next.

They'd been on the road for nearly three hours at this point. Bear had done his best to snake this way and that, throwing off anyone trying to keep an eye on him. He knew the car was clean, and he had checked his and Cara's clothes, ensuring neither of them had a tracker.

Rodger would undoubtedly check again.

Bear roused Cara from her slumber as he took the offramp for a rest stop. It was the kind that only had a handful of bathrooms, a couple vending machines, and a single picnic table. That's where Goldstone was waiting for them.

"Tuck your hair inside your hat. Go use the bathroom. Get me a coffee and grab some snacks." He handed her wad of ones and then pointed at the table. "Then meet me over there."

"Is that him?" she asked, pressing her face against the glass of the window.

"That's him," Bear said, unable to control the mix of apprehension and resolution that filled his voice. "From this point forward, we have to be ready."

Cara turned back to him, confusion written all over her face. "For what?"

Bear popped his door open and stood up out of the car. Cara followed suit. He took a moment to stretch his legs and shoot one more look in Goldstone's direction before he answered her.

"For anything."

19

BEAR WAITED UNTIL CARA WAS INSIDE THE REST STOP BUILDING before he approached Goldstone. It had been years since he'd last seen the man, but he didn't look any older, any wearier. Maybe he was onto something about farm life.

Bear stopped at the corner of the table. "Sir."

"Riley." Goldstone had a deeply southern accent that was both regal and commanding. You couldn't help but listen to what he had to say. "You got a mess going on here."

"That I do." Bear sat down across from the old man. "I appreciate your help."

Goldstone waved him off. "Saw your name as soon as it popped up. Didn't believe it for a second."

"I appreciate that more than you know."

"Been keeping an eye on you and Jack over the years. Can't say I approve of everything you've done, but...I can't say I don't either."

Bear wasn't sure what to say. He doubted Goldstone had the time to follow-up on many people from his past. "Why us?"

Goldstone shrugged, the corner of his lips lifting in the

process. "Professional interests. You two were the biggest pains in my ass back in the day. I was pretty sure you were going to make something of yourselves."

"Jack would be happy to hear that."

"Where is Noble anyway? He was as slippery as a greased hog, that one."

Bear chuckled. "He's laying low. You heard about Germany?"

"I did." Goldstone looked contemplative. "You two sure have been stirring up the pot lately."

"Unintentional," Bear said, holding up his hands. "We didn't know what we were getting into."

"I believe it." Goldstone shifted, and Bear followed his gaze. Cara was headed toward them now. "I expect the full story when we get home. First, I need to know we can trust her."

"She's in as deep as I am."

"Not what I asked you, son."

It was funny how a single word out of the man's mouth could make Bear sit a little straighter. "She won't tell me the name of her informant. I think it's someone well-positioned in the White House. Male. Other than that, from what I can tell, she's been upfront about everything. She understands the stakes. She cares about this story, about doing what's right. But she's green. She's capable of making stupid mistakes."

Goldstone leveled a look at Bear. It took every ounce of strength not to wither underneath it. "Aren't we all?"

Cara approached the table and waved sheepishly at the two of them.

Goldstone stood and extended his hand toward her. "Ms. Bishop, my name is Rodger. Riley tells me you're a damn fine reporter. I only got the basics from our phone conversation, but it sounds like you singlehandedly blew this case wide open."

"I had a lot of help," Cara said, shaking the man's hand. "Especially from *Riley* here."

Bear ignored her jab and stood. "I think it's best if we get going."

"First things first," Goldstone said. He pulled a device from his pocket. "Phones on the table, please."

Bear and Cara complied. Goldstone swept them for bugs, getting no hits in return. Bear was glad he hadn't missed anything when he'd done his initial inspection of their clothes.

When Cara reached for her phone, Goldstone waved a finger at her. "I'm afraid that won't do, Ms. Bishop."

"It was part of the deal," Bear said. He'd purposely withheld that bit of information from her. "We can't risk being tracked to the farm."

"I need to be able to get into contact with my informant."

"I'm sorry, Ms. Bishop," Goldstone said, his voice gentle but firm. "Either the phone stays, or you do."

There was no arguing with that. Cara nodded her head, and Bear disassembled both their phones, dropping the pieces in different garbage cans along the way. He felt a sense of relief now. They were truly off the grid. No one would know they were at Goldstone's farm. Even just the idea of getting a few days to regroup was reinvigorating for Bear. He wouldn't be able to sleep right now if he tried.

Instead, he spent the next three hours filling Goldstone in on every detail of the situation so far while riding shotgun in his old Ford truck. Bear started back in Costa Rica, then jumped to Korea, then London. Every time he mentioned Thorne, Goldstone clicked his tongue disapprovingly. When Bear finally asked him about it, Goldstone just shook his head and said Thorne wouldn't know what loyalty was if it danced the Merengue in nothing but unmentionables.

For the most part, Cara was quiet in the back seat. Bear would bet money she was itching to write down some of the details of what he said. He was sure she didn't know much of the details of what happened in Korea. It had occurred to him it would be dangerous to let her in on that government secret, but then he realized that you couldn't really get into any more trouble than they already were. What was one more clandestine operation?

Goldstone asked questions where he needed more clarification, but for the most part, he just let Bear talk. It felt good to get the sequence of events out there. He'd been holding it in for so long. The only people he had truly been able to talk to about it had been Jack and Sadie, but they'd mostly been there with him. Telling Goldstone was like seeing everything from a fresh perspective.

Bear was just getting into his chat with Jack in Germany when they pulled down a long dirt road. Stones kicked up by the tires pinged at the underside of Goldstone's truck. It was a bumpy, dusty drive. Trees along the driveway blocked the house from view. When it finally appeared beyond a small hill, Bear completely understood why Goldstone had retired here.

His house was moderate, but still conveyed a sense of strength. It was stark white with deep red shutters. The door matched. Sitting out front was a much nicer car than the Ford. Did it belong to his wife? Did he use it to meet with his government contacts? Bear couldn't imagine Goldstone sitting behind the wheel of that vehicle when he looked so comfortable behind the wheel of this one.

The fields were sprawling. Beyond the house was a huge swath of corn. In another area, a group of cows gathered, munching on grass. A barn rose up in the distance, and Bear wondered how many other animals made their home there.

Cara's voice came from the back. "Do you live alone, Mr. Goldstone?"

"Please, call me Rodger." Goldstone pulled the truck up to the house and threw it in park. "I live with my wife, daughter, and my granddaughter. Lots of estrogen around these parts, but I wouldn't have it any other way."

"Are they here?" Bear asked, looking up at the house.

"I sent them to go stay with my sister for a few days. I hope you understand why."

"I don't blame you."

"Let's get you guys fed, shall we? The missus left us a roast."

Bear's stomach growled right on command, and the three of them jumped out of the truck and marched up the stairs and into Goldstone's house. As rustic as the whole place was, Bear didn't miss the array of surveillance devices. Cameras littered his property. Some of them were obvious if you knew where to look. Bear was sure there were dozens he'd never be able to find.

Goldstone's lock was also state of the art. It required a keycode and a fingerprint. Bear wouldn't be surprised if his security system cost hundreds of thousands of dollars. It made him wonder if it was for his family alone, or if Goldstone was keeping state secrets here as well.

Bear and Cara sat at the dining room table as Goldstone put together a plate for each of them. He also offered them each whiskey, and Bear was surprised when Cara knocked hers back like a pro. For the first time, he considered that she was more seasoned than she looked. After all, he had never asked. What had she seen in the few years she'd been a reporter? Considering how well she was handling this story, Bear was forced to admit that it might be more than he originally thought.

As they were wiping their plates clean and groaning in satisfaction, Goldstone looked at Bear out of the corner of his eye. "You never said who it was."

"Who what was?"

"Don't play coy with me, Riley. That was always Jack's job."

Bear laughed. "He was damn good at it, too."

"Not as good as you might think."

Bear laughed again, but this one was short-lived. He'd avoided naming the Director of National Intelligence for a reason. He didn't know the kind of relationship Goldstone had with the man, but it was likely that the two knew each other. Maybe they were friendly. Maybe they were just colleagues. But Bear had trusted Goldstone up until this point. What was one more piece of information?

"You're asking who's behind all of this? Who's coordinating these attacks?"

"That I am."

Bear took one more sip of his whiskey. "Mason Hughes."

Goldstone took a few seconds to absorb the information, then he wiped his mouth with his napkin, threw it down on the table, and stood up to his full height.

"I knew that son of a bitch would cross the line sooner or later, and I vowed I'd be there when it happened." He crossed the room and put a hand on the knob of a door that seemed to lead to the basement, looking back over his shoulder. "Follow me. I've got some information you might find useful."

20

BEAR AND CARA EXCHANGED A LOOK AND THEN PUSHED BACK FROM the table. Bear led the way to the door and then down the stairs. At the bottom was a thick steel door with another hi-tech security keypad and fingerprint reader. Bear slipped through the opening, not the least surprised that Goldstone had a bunker in his basement. He was surprised, however, by how small it was.

Goldstone must've seen the look on his face.

"This is only the foyer," he said. "You'll have to trust me on the rest."

"Understood."

Cara walked up beside him, her eyes wide with curiosity. Not for the first time, Bear wondered what she made of this entire situation. She was taking it all in stride, but despite her adaptive personality, she'd probably never been through something like this before. It tends to change you forever. He wondered if she'd realized that yet.

"These computers serve a dual purpose," Goldstone said in his signature drawl. "One, they track all the security footage I have and store it on a server far away from here. They say the best line of defense is a good offense, but I like to make sure my defense is nice and strong, too."

"What's the second purpose?" Cara asked.

"Keeping track of every secret I've ever learned over the course of my career."

Bear blanched. "That's a lot of information."

Goldstone tipped his head. "It is."

"A lot of people won't like the fact that you've written it all down."

"They won't." Goldstone turned and pecked away at the keyboard in front of him. "I've found it to be pretty good insurance over the years. Not a lot of people know I've taken my work home with me, so to speak, but those that do know that I don't bluff."

"What kind of security you got on this?" Bear asked. He wasn't necessarily a tech guy, but he knew state-of-the-art when he saw it.

"The best of the best. Made friends with a nice young man around the time I was set to retire. Absolute genius when it came to computers. He set me up for success and stays on top of all the latest developments in the field. I get updates before the Pentagon does."

"That sounds expensive," Cara said. The question was implied.

"I had a very good retirement package." Goldstone turned around and put his hands on his hips. "Are you sure this is Hughes? I'm not askin' because I don't believe you. I'm askin' because I want to make sure you've got your sights set on the right beast."

"All signs point to yes," Bear said. "Even if he's not the one behind this whole scheme, he's one of the major players."

"I've known Mason Hughes for a long time. We're contemporaries. We never ran in the same circles, but we've shared a few drinks over the years. Never liked the guy. He was ambitious in a way that didn't sit right with me. He was willing to cut corners. As much as I hate to say it, sometimes the job calls for that. But this was different. He enjoyed taking the low road. Winnin' was his only concern."

"Why did you start tracking him?"

Goldstone chuckled. "I had a lot of different reasons. The fact that he was the Director of National Intelligence didn't hurt. Someone like that having the President's ear? Hughes cares about this country, no doubt about it. I do think he serves to ensure we always come out on top. I gotta respect that mentality. But I knew sooner or later he was gonna put more than just a toe over that invisible line we all agreed not to cross."

Cara spoke for the first time. "Do you have anything that can connect him to Mateo and the bombings in Europe?"

Goldstone clucked his tongue. "Not directly. Hughes is smart. He'll have several people in between him and those doing the dirty work. The communications will be secure and encrypted. They'll probably use a code, and not one that could be easily broken."

"Why do I feel like there's a *but* coming?" Bear asked.

Goldstone held a finger up to the side of his nose and smiled. "Like I said, I've been keeping an eye on Hughes for some time now. I'm not the only one who was concerned about how far his loyalty to this country would take him. We're all patriots, but some of us don't have the blind faith Hughes has. That blind faith raised a few flags with a couple of us."

"Who else is worried about him?" Cara asked.

Goldstone waggled a finger in her direction. "You've got a good nose for reporting. You know the questions to ask. But I'm not going to answer that one, Ms. Bishop. It's better you don't know."

Cara deflated a little bit, but Bear could also see the pride shining through. She enjoyed her job, reveled in it the way Bear did in his. That sort of passion would take her places. If it didn't get her killed first.

Goldstone turned back to the computer and pulled up a grainy black and white photo of a group of men. It looked to be from security footage, and not a very good device at that. Bear stepped forward and squinted. One of the men looked remarkably like Goldstone. He didn't know most of the others, until his eyes landed on Senator Goddard.

"Where did you get this?" Bear asked.

"Hughes' schedule put him at a golf meeting in Florida with Vice President Eli Adams and a few lucky business owners who would have their attention for a couple of hours. Normally, I wouldn't have flagged this at all, but the Vice President and Hughes don't exactly see eye to eye. Adams is a bit passive for Hughes, a little too cautious. The two have been known to butt heads."

"What businesses did the other men own?"

Goldstone flashed a smile again. "Another excellent question, Ms. Bishop. One of the business owners happened to be none other than your dead friend Mateo. The other men attending their little golf tournament were friends of Mateo's. One is in the hospitality business, one owns several private airfields around the country, and the third was former military-turned-entrepreneur. He deals in cell phones now."

"So, travel, communications, and lodging are all covered," Bear said.

Goldstone nodded. "My thoughts exactly. The gathering was supposedly business off-limits, but we all know how these things go. Everyone's got an ulterior motive."

"Do you think the Vice President is in on it?" Cara asked.

"I never say never," Goldstone responded, "but I would be surprised. When I say the relationship between Adams and

Hughes is contentious, I mean it. As far as I heard, it didn't sit well that Hughes missed out on their little game."

Bear looked back down at the picture. "Why didn't he make the meeting?"

"It seems he was called away to Costa Rica. I couldn't tell you why. I can tell you, however, that he met with Goddard while he was there." Goldstone pointed at the two men in the picture. "All security footage was wiped out in a two-block radius of this meeting. In fact, anywhere Hughes went, all video and audio feeds mysteriously malfunctioned. It seems Hughes didn't want anyone knowing where he had gone."

"How did you get this picture then?" Bear asked.

Goldstone chuckled. "It's from a bakery that just installed a hidden camera. Someone was robbing his shop at least once a week. He hadn't told anyone he'd installed it. Spent a pretty penny on the camera, too. Not that you could tell from the quality of the image. I sent a local man around to doublecheck that nothing had been left behind. Turns out the owner trusts his own people more than foreign governments. Who knew? He was more than willing to let my guy look through the footage."

"Did he catch them?" Cara asked.

Both Bear and Goldstone looked at her.

She looked from one to the other. "The person who was robbing him. Did the owner catch them?"

"I believe it was his own daughter," Goldstone said, "stealing money and pies to give to her secret lover. I can't say I know how the story ends, though I assume it is not well—for either one of them."

Cara seemed satisfied with the answer, so Bear turned back to the monitor. "What else do you have?"

There was a twinkle in Goldstone's eye. "Everything you need."

21

It turned out that Director Hughes had been a busy man over the last year or so. Though Goldstone didn't have any hard proof of it, he had taken note that the government official had booked a trip to South Korea before he canceled it at the last minute.

Bear had asked if there was any connection between Hughes and Thorne, but Goldstone wasn't able to provide anything concrete. The two had met and worked together in the past, though this wasn't out of the ordinary. With Hughes being the Director of National Intelligence and Thorne being one of the country's best operatives, it was bound to happen. However, they didn't seem chummy outside of work hours. Or, at least, as far as Goldstone's records showed.

Hughes had been in London when the bomb nearly went off. Goldstone had pinpointed his location, and it seemed that their esteemed DNI would have been just outside the blast radius, but still close enough to cause at least some panic on his behalf. Bear was sure that had been a calculated move. No one would suspect someone who had gotten caught up in one of the disasters. Plus, the PR from a near death experience would have been great for the cause. It also would've given Hughes motive to go on the offensive, making the enactment of this little plan all the easier.

Bear got some satisfaction from the fact that he had probably ruined Hughes' plan—or at least set him back one or two steps. Keeping that bomb from going off had saved countless lives, but it had also lessened the impact of Hughes' grand scheme. Knowing there had been a bomb was different than experiencing it explode. People forgot one a lot faster than they forgot the other.

"What about Germany?" Bear asked.

Goldstone scrolled through his notes until he got to the bottom. "I don't have anything on that. Hughes was in D.C. when it happened. There's nothing here that ties him to it."

Cara slipped a handful of folded papers from her pocket. "What do you make of this?"

When Goldstone unraveled the stack, Bear realized it was the blueprints to the bomb. She must've found them in his jacket after all. When Bear lifted an eyebrow at her, she just smiled and shrugged her shoulders.

"These are some interesting specs," Goldstone said, flipping through the pages. "It would definitely get past security, but I don't know how reliable it would be."

"What do you mean?" Cara asked.

"Imagine you're a terrorist. You want to send twenty guys out to plant bombs all over the world using this blueprint for the devices. You have to manufacture these parts and get them in the hands of your people. Then you have to trust they'll be able to keep ahold of them. Not to mention assemble the bomb, place it, and then detonate it. It's a little more complicated than strapping some C4 to your chest and walking into the middle of a crowd to press a button."

"Hughes is capable of that," Bear offered. "He'd be able to coordinate all this."

"But is he?" Cara asked. "You guys said it yourself, Hughes has been trying to keep his distance. Whatever is going on here, he's trying to keep several people in between him and the bombs."

"Especially now that the London bomb didn't go off," Bear added, "and he didn't get to play the victim—or the hero."

"We need a trail," Cara said. "We can draw a line between Mateo and Hughes. We can also draw a line between Hughes and everything you've been through, Bear. But that's all retrospective. We need something that puts his finger on the trigger of the Germany bomb and anything else that comes out of his plan to start another World War."

"Then we need to find the next bomb." Bear turned to Goldstone. "You got any ideas where Hughes is heading next? Any phone calls he's made to foreign powers? Anything at all to give us a clue where to start looking?"

Goldstone turned back to his computer and started clicking away on his keyboard. The room was silent other than the sound of his typing. Cara was still studying the blueprints. Bear was looking around the bunker, wondering what it looked like beyond these four walls.

When Goldstone turned around, his face said everything. "I've got nothing. As far as I can tell, Hughes isn't going anywhere. His official schedule indicates he's locked up in D.C. He's going to be using secure lines of communication for all his private dealings. We won't be able to crack that."

Bear held up a finger. "I wouldn't be so sure about that. I've got a guy."

"He better be one of the best."

Bear grinned. "He is."

Cara put down the schematics for the bomb and looked at Bear. "I need to get something into the hands of my editor."

"No way," Bear said. "Too dangerous."

"I understand the risks." Cara's voice was even. She was in journalist mode now. "But think about it. If I start connecting the dots, it'll force Hughes into action. He'll have to move up his timetable. He might get sloppy. We can use that to our advantage."

"If you publish something, he'll come down on you with the entire force of the United States. If he can't find you, he'll start hauling in your family."

Cara waved off the comment. "I don't have any family. And he's already after me. This isn't going to change that."

Goldstone's voice was gentle. "Sweetheart, there's a lot more the Director of National Intelligence can do to you. Trust me on that."

Cara's mask cracked ever so slightly, but she stood resolute. "This will help us get the ball rolling. My editor knows what I've been working on. He'll see that I'm being called a murderer. He's a smart guy. He's got my back. He'll know I'm innocent."

"Would you bet your life on it?" Bear asked.

Cara's answer was immediate. "I would."

Goldstone and Bear exchanged a look.

The journalist let out a heavy sigh. "Look, I know how this works. If I send something to my editor, he has a right to publish it. He must also turn in any evidence in the case against me. We'll send it from a random city on our way back east. They won't be able to track it."

Bear didn't love the idea, but he couldn't argue with her points. "Why do I feel like there's something else going on here?"

Cara looked sheepish. "My contact can no longer reach me by cell. We have a backup plan, but that's only when we're ready to blow this whole thing wide open. I think we have enough here to get started. My source will be able to fill in some of the blanks."

Goldstone opened his mouth, but Bear held up a hand. "Don't bother asking. She won't tell you."

Cara just grinned.

Bear and Goldstone exchanged another look, and this time, it was Goldstone who broke the silence. "The two of you are welcome to stay here for the night. I don't suggest you hang around any longer than that. Best to keep moving."

Bear extended his hand. "I appreciate your help, Rodger. And your faith in me."

"Both come easy," Goldstone said, shaking Bear's hand, "though let's not make a habit out of it."

"Where's the fun in that?"

"You'd be surprised, young man." Goldstone's eyes twinkled. "Plenty of fun in a life spent at home with a family."

Something tugged at Bear's heart, but he ignored it. "I'll have to trust you on that."

"What else do you two need before we hit the sack for the night?"

"A shower?" Cara asked.

"A secure phone line," Bear said.

"I got 'em both," Goldstone replied.

Bear's former commanding officer pointed him to a landline before taking Cara upstairs and showing her their accommodations. Bear waited until they were out of earshot before dialing a number he knew by heart.

"Brandon? It's Bear. I have a little project for you."

22

THE NEXT MORNING, EVERYONE AT THE GOLDSTONE RESIDENCE WOKE up with the sun. Cara didn't complain nearly as much as the first time they had to do that, and Bear wondered if it was because her body was already adjusting to the new routine or because she didn't want to draw attention from Rodger Goldstone.

The three of them ate a hearty breakfast, mostly in silence. They had said everything they'd needed to last night, and Goldstone wasn't one to dwell on gratitude. One *thank you* was enough. Everyone there knew how much he was risking just by putting them up for a single night. No use in wasting more time groveling.

"I've got a truck you can borrow," Goldstone said. "It needs a little tune-up, but it'll get you where you need to go. Even got some plates registered under a fake name."

"What if you need the backup plan?" Bear asked.

"I don't need it more than you do right now." Goldstone stood and gathered their plates. "Having that truck around makes the missus feel better. I'll have to get us a new one, but she'll understand."

"Tell her thanks," Bear said. He'd never met Goldstone's wife, but from what he'd heard over the years, she'd put up with a lot of the bullshit that came with her husband's career and never once thought about giving up on him. Not a lot of people could be that supportive from the sidelines.

Cara drained the rest of her orange juice and handed the glass to Goldstone. "Do you have a pen and some paper?"

"That I do, Ms. Bishop. Follow me." Goldstone paused in the doorway. "Riley, go fetch the toolbox in the barn. Meet me in the building behind the cornfield. We'll get that truck looked over."

Bear stepped out into the cool morning air and took a deep breath. It was mid-November and you could smell winter on the wind. There was a crispness that would turn to snow sooner rather than later. He wondered where he'd be when it finally hit. New York? Someplace warmer? Maybe he'd be in a cell. Or maybe he'd be in the ground.

It wasn't the most optimistic thought, but it was a realistic one. Bear's head was full of conflicting thoughts as he made his way to the barn to grab the toolbox. Part of him wanted to cut anchor and run. He'd have a better chance of survival that way.

But another part of him wanted to see this thing through. For his sake and Jack's. And Cara Bishop. She deserved to live out the rest of her life. When Bear thought about how much of the world she probably hadn't seen yet, he couldn't help but feel bitter. There were thousands of Cara Bishops out there, like the girl he'd rescued in Germany. One man decided to ruin all their lives because he had some sort of savior complex.

Bear pulled the barn door open and was met with a mixture of hay and manure that was both pungent and somehow relaxing. It smelled like long days of hard work and the kind of exhaustion that made you proud to be alive.

A single horse was in its stall, along with a cluster of sheep on one side. Bear spotted the toolbox right away and made a beeline for it. Seeing the animals, and the horse especially, made Bear consider, for maybe the first time in his life, what it would be like to live like this. Off the grid. Self-sufficient. Away from people and the problems they create.

But he didn't have time to think like that.

Instead, he grabbed the toolbox and hauled it across Goldstone's property. He cut through the cornfield, careful not to trample any of the stalks, and found himself face to face with a medium-sized shed. When Bear pulled the doors open, he was met with a black Chevy Silverado.

There was cracking and crunching from behind Bear, and when he turned, he saw Goldstone making his way through the field.

"It's about eight years old at this point, but she runs just fine."

Bear looked down at the toolbox in his hands and then up at Goldstone again.

"You thought I would've let my getaway car get rusty? Maybe you don't know me as well as you think you do."

"A ruse," Bear said. "What's this really about then?"

"Always good to do a maintenance check before an undetermined amount of time on the road. Wasn't a complete ruse. Pop the hood for me?"

Bear set down the box and opened the hood of the truck. Everything looked good at a glance, but he was grateful to get in there anyway. Better to know what he was working with than get surprised on the highway when everything started shutting down.

"What I really wanted to know—," Goldstone grunted as he leaned over the engine with a flashlight in one hand, "—was why you're doing this."

If Bear believed in that sort of thing, he would've thought

Goldstone had heard his thoughts all the way from the barn. "Don't really have a choice."

Goldstone threw him a look and then returned to the job at hand. "We all have a choice. You more than most. You have the ability to disappear. You can go up to Canada or down to Mexico and find a new life to live. But you want to keep this one."

"Don't really like the idea of being on the run for the rest of my life," Bear said.

"That's the ticket. Why else?"

Bear shifted from one foot to another. He felt like Goldstone was the teacher who had singled him out in front of the class. Bear didn't have the answer, but he was being forced to work through the problem anyway. Goldstone wasn't exactly the kind of instructor who would accept anything less than what Bear was capable of.

"Jack. The girl." Bear paused for the briefest of seconds. "Because it's the right thing to do."

"Jack would be fine on his own. We both know that." Goldstone began to move around the vehicle now, checking it from all sides. "I like Ms. Bishop. She reminds me of my daughter."

"Oh?"

"Stubborn as a mule." He chuckled. "Likes to stick her nose where it doesn't belong."

"That doesn't exactly sound like a compliment."

Goldstone finished circling the truck and clicked off the flashlight. "Oh, it is. Those are the kinds of people you want to keep close by. They're a pain in the ass nine times out of ten, but it's that tenth time that'll save your life."

Bear laughed. He couldn't argue with that. "Noted."

"Are you sure this is the right thing to do?" Goldstone asked. Bear got the sense that a simple *yes* wouldn't be enough of an answer.

"We can't let Hughes get away with this. He's supposed to be protecting this country."

"Maybe he is," Goldstone offered. "Maybe this is his way of doing exactly that."

Bear's face twisted into a grimace. "Are you defending him?"

"No, sir." Goldstone's voice was light and even. "Just presenting another perspective."

"Killing innocent people to protect innocent people doesn't seem like the right solution to our problems."

"Can't say I disagree."

Bear ran a hand down his face. "I'm in a position to do something about it."

"You are."

"So, I have to."

"You don't."

Bear was getting tired of the cryptic questioning. "You going to tell me what this is about?"

Goldstone crossed his arms over his chest. "I was going to ask you the same thing. Something's holding you back. Something is making you hesitate. I'm trying to get you to admit what it is before that hesitation gets you killed."

"I'm just tired of it, you know?" The words came before Bear could stop them. "The conspiracies, the betrayals, the running and hiding. It's been full tilt since Costa Rica, except for those couple of months on the island. I'd never been happier."

"So, you want to give it all up?"

"Sometimes."

"I've had that thought more times than I can count. Want to know what conclusion I end up coming to every single time?"

Bear nodded.

"Those island moments can only exist in contrast to every moment spent hunkered down behind a sandbag, trading shots with the enemy." Goldstone uncrossed his arms and tossed the flashlight back in the toolbox. "If you lived those island moments every day for the rest of your life, they wouldn't be so precious."

Bear didn't have a retort. He knew Goldstone was right. He also knew that he'd be bored out of his mind if he retired early. That was probably why Goldstone had stayed on as a consultant in D.C. He wasn't in on the action anymore, but he wasn't completely out of it either.

"How did you make it this far?" Bear hated the desperation in his voice, like he needed the answer to this question to get through the next few days. He cleared his throat and tried again. "You've served longer than anyone else I know. How did you get through all that?"

Goldstone didn't hesitate. "It was mostly luck and skill."

"Mostly?"

"And I came to an important realization." Goldstone paused, making sure he had Bear's undivided attention. "Most people come back from war and claim they saw the worst of humanity. I never felt that way. I always felt like I saw the best of it."

Bear didn't answer. He couldn't.

"A lot of terrible things happen in the world. Every day, there seems to be something new. We tend to focus on the negative, on the tragedy. I'm not sure why. Maybe it confirms what we already think we know—that humans are terrible creatures, hellbent on death and destruction."

Goldstone turned around and slammed the Silverado's hood shut. He closed up the toolbox and took one last look at the truck before turning back to Bear.

"It's a lot harder to believe in people. To have that kind of trust in another human being means you have to be vulnerable, and nobody likes doing that." He chuckled. "But we have to. Otherwise, what's the point?"

Bear finally found his voice. "Are you telling me to trust the girl?"

Goldstone clapped a hand on Bear's shoulder. "And Jack. And me. And yourself."

"You don't think I trust myself?"

"Few people do. From the second you walked back into my life, I saw how much you were battling yourself. I said it once, and I'll say it again, that kind of hesitation will get you killed. Either commit or don't. Only you can decide."

Bear couldn't argue with that. So, he didn't.

"Anyway," Goldstone said, removing his hand from Bear's shoulder. "The truck is yours. Whatever you do, just be smart about it. And try not to wreck her? She's only been in the outside world a couple times. Be gentle."

23

GOLDSTONE HAD GIVEN BEAR INSTRUCTIONS TO HEAD TO NEW Glarus, Wisconsin. It was a small town about two hours south, near the Illinois border. Even when Cara's letters were eventually traced back to there, it wouldn't indicate where they had been or which direction they had been heading in. From Chicago to New Glarus, they could have been going anywhere.

The Silverado ran smoothly. Bear was glad to be in something bigger and newer than the Camry. Out here in farm country, they'd blend right in. If they ended up heading to New York or D.C., on the other hand, they'd have a hard time disappearing into the crowd.

For her part, Cara remained quiet on the road to New Glarus. She sat with a stack of papers in her lap, reading and re-reading what she'd written. Occasionally, she'd cross off a word and scribble in a new one. She cursed every time they hit a bump and her pen made a mark across the page.

Bear didn't interrupt her thoughts until they were nearly at their destination. He cleared his throat and waited for her to look up. Her eyes were bleary with the strain of staring at her writing for so long.

Bear cracked a smile. "You trying to win a Pulitzer over there?"

"It has to be perfect." She was deadly serious. "No misinformation. No mistakes. I have to make sure it's good enough to publish."

Bear nodded. A lot was riding on this. It was meant to be the first step in clearing their names. It was meant to push Hughes and his men into doing something stupid. And it was meant to tell the general public that there was a lot more going on here than they realized.

"Do you want to read it to me?" he asked.

Cara blinked. "You wouldn't mind?"

Bear just shrugged his shoulders. If he was being honest, he needed to know what she had written down. She was right—one wrong word could spell disaster for either one of them. They needed to be more careful than ever from here on out. No slip-ups. No distractions.

Cara shifted in her seat. She sat a little taller. Then she began reading. Her voice took on a different tone, a different cadence. This wasn't just Cara Bishop. It was Cara Bishop, the reporter. Her words were even, and Bear could tell she had chosen each one with purpose.

She didn't name names, but she spoke of a government conspiracy that aimed to promote green technology while using it as a front to create a new kind of weapon, all with the aim of disrupting foreign societies with the hopes of controlling them.

But Cara didn't linger on that. Instead, she focused on the meeting with Mateo, the one she wasn't even meant to be at. She described her fear and anguish over hearing him murdered, and her subsequent confusion when it was ultimately pinned on her.

Cara had a way of writing that pulled at the heartstrings. She used facts and turned them into emotion. Bear had been with her for nearly the entire journey, and yet this was the first time he had really seen the events from her perspective.

When she finished, silence hung in the air.

"I liked it," Bear said. The words seemed simple, almost grotesque compared to hers. "But you forgot one important detail."

Cara looked back down at the paper, searching for where she could've missed something. "What?"

"You never mentioned the knight in shining armor who saved you."

Cara looked over at him and rolled her eyes. "I thought it was best to leave you out. You're already in enough trouble as it is."

"I appreciate it. Doesn't matter now anyway." Bear pointed at the approaching sign in front of them. "We're here."

Cara leaned forward to get a better look at New Glarus, but there wasn't much to see. The sign welcoming them to the town stated the population was just over two thousand. The idea was that few people would be paying attention to big city Chicago news, at least compared to somewhere like Madison or Milwaukee.

But Bear knew better than most that even small towns could bring big trouble.

He drove through town once just to get the lay of the land. It was pretty simple, with most everything clustered in the downtown area. He decided to park at the other end of town on a side road that looked like it didn't get much traffic. No one would bother the truck, and he could control who did and did not see him get back into it.

The hardest part would be convincing Cara to stay behind.

"No," she said, as soon as he told her his plan. "No way. I'm going with you."

"You can't."

"I can. And I will. This is my story."

Bear shifted in his seat to look at her directly. "I know this is important to you. I know how much this means to you. But you have to trust me. If we both go out there together, our chances of being recognized double, at the very least. We can't risk it."

"So, I'll go alone."

Bear smiled. "That's dangerous."

"I can handle myself."

"I don't doubt that. But I've gotta take this one for the team. If I'm spotted, I'll be able to slip away or take out anyone who gets bold. It's not about what you can't do."

Cara tipped her head back and sighed. "And you'll come right back?"

"I promise." Bear unbuckled his seat belt and held out his hand for the papers. "I'll be walking directly to the post office and then directly back."

Cara handed over the papers without even looking at him. "Fine."

"Tip your seat back until it's flat. Close your eyes and try to get a couple minutes in. You won't even know I'm gone."

Cara didn't respond. Instead, she let her hand drop to the side of the seat and started lowering the back until it was parallel with the floor of the truck. No one would be able to see her unless they walked right up to the window and looked in.

"I'm leaving you with the keys," Bear said. "In case you need to get out of here."

That snapped her back to attention. She sat bolt upright. "What? No. I'm not going to leave you."

"If someone sees you, drive south to the next town. I'll meet you there." When Cara opened her mouth to argue some more, Bear held up a hand. "That's the plan. Stick to it. Lock the doors when I'm out. Don't open up for anyone else, even if they say they know me."

Cara crossed her arms over her chest, which Bear took as a sign of her reluctant acceptance. He patted her on the shoulder and jumped out of the truck. When he shut the door, he waited until she locked up before he started his trek into town.

The temperature had dropped another ten degrees since yesterday. Bear was grateful Goldstone had given him a winter jacket to wear. It barely stretched across his broad shoulders, but it was enough to keep him warm, even if he couldn't zip it up.

Bear threw a look over his shoulder and noticed Cara still watching him walk away. When he caught her eyes, she dropped down and out of sight. Bear breathed a sigh of relief. If he was quick, they likely wouldn't run into any trouble. Then he could hop back on the road and figure out their next destination.

He tucked her papers under his arm and set a steady pace toward the center of town. He wasn't sure her story would do much—there was still a chance it wouldn't even get printed—but he knew they had to try. Anything to put another roadblock in Hughes' plan was good enough for him.

Bear kept a watchful eye out. In a town like this, locals would notice a stranger right away. Was he just passing through or was he new in town? Bear didn't plan on sticking around long enough to answer those sorts of questions, but he knew he had to be ready either way.

The streets were quiet until he was nearly to the center of town. Families gathered together, entering or leaving the local diner. Couples shared a coffee on a park bench. Dog owners walked their furry friends from tree to tree, waiting them to do something, anything, so they could go back inside to the warmth of their houses.

Bear made a beeline for the post office. It was a small, square building without much flair. When he pulled open the door, a bell chimed, and everyone inside looked at him. There was a tense moment where they each tried to place him. When they couldn't, they either looked away, or turned toward their friend to whisper in hushed tones.

Everyone except for the sheriff, of course.

He was second in line, dropping off a rectangular package. He kept staring at Bear, who nodded cordially and then walked over to the rack of envelopes against one of the walls. He could still feel the officer's eyes on the back of his head, but Bear didn't let it distract him.

In and out, that was the plan.

Bear selected a sturdy padded envelope for Cara's papers and slid them inside. He grabbed a pen and copied the address she had given him on the front of the package, careful to write legibly. He then sealed it shut and turned to join the line.

The sheriff had engaged the person behind him in conversation, giving him the perfect opportunity to keep an eye on Bear.

For his part, Bear didn't bother making eye contact.

The line moved slowly. That was the problem with small towns. Everyone knew everyone and wanted to know everyone's business. The woman who had been at the front of the line when Bear walked in was still chit-chatting with the man behind the counter. They were moving at a snail's pace, though no one seemed to care except Bear.

When the two of them finally said their goodbyes, the mailman had to call the sheriff by name three times before he realized he was up next.

"Sorry about that, Sam," said Sheriff Daniels. "I was off in a whole other world."

"Don't bother me none, sir. How's the wife?"

"Oh, she's good, she's good. Got her hands full with the little ones."

"How old are they now?"

"Nine and twelve."

"Sara's almost a teenager now!"

"Don't remind me, Sam. Don't remind me." Sheriff Daniels chuckled. "Gets away with everything She's already got me wrapped around her finger. And knows it, too! I'm hopeless."

The women behind the sheriff sighed as though they wished their husbands were as doting. Bear wondered if the sheriff was hamming it up or if he really was that much of a family man. If he had to place bets, it was the former. His position was appointed, which meant that public opinion meant everything.

Bear tuned them out after that. The sheriff spent a good five minutes talking to Sam the mailman after he dropped off his package. When he left, he paused at the door and stared long and hard at Bear. For his part, Bear didn't return the favor. Better to look oblivious.

Another fifteen minutes passed before it was Bear's turn at the counter. He stayed cordial, but kept his answers short. When Sam finally realized he wouldn't be able to get anything out of Bear, he smiled and sent him on his way.

When Bear exited the building and saw the sheriff sitting on the hood of his vehicle, Bear knew that any plan he had to get in and out of New Glarus had just gone out the window.

24

"Mornin'." The sheriff didn't wait for Bear to respond. "Don't think I've seen you 'round here before."

"I'm just passing through," Bear said. He kept his tone friendly but didn't linger.

"Where you comin' from, if you don't mind me asking?"

He did mind, but refusing to give the officer an answer would only make things worse. "Up north."

"Madison?"

"Little further than that." Bear was almost out of reasonable earshot now. He decided to try his luck at getting away. "Have a good day, sheriff."

Bear knew he couldn't head directly back to the truck without leading the other man to Cara and thus increasing their chances of being recognized. Instead, he made a beeline for the local diner and took up a spot at the counter.

A portly waitress with a tired smile on her face welcomed Bear as he sat down in front of her at the counter. "What can I get for you, sugar?"

"Coffee, please."

"Lookin' for any breakfast? We got a combo platter that'll fill you up nice and easy."

"No, ma'am." Bear wasn't planning on staying long. "Just need some caffeine before I get back on the road."

The waitress grabbed a mug and a pot of coffee and poured Bear a cup. "Where're you headed?"

Why were people in small towns so nosy? "South."

"Lots of things to the south," she said.

Bear shrugged. "I stop when something catches my eye."

The waitress batted her eyelashes, but Bear took a sip of coffee and looked away.

Just in time to see the sheriff walk through the door.

He sat down next to Bear with a stool in between them. "Don't think I caught your name earlier."

Bear's reply was quick and easy. "John."

"You got a last name, John?"

The hair on the back of Bear's neck was starting to stand on end. "Yes, sir, I do."

"You're not much of a talker, are you, John?"

"No, sir, I'm not. Especially when it comes to strangers. Even if they're wearing a badge."

Tension hung in the air for a few seconds before Sheriff Daniels barked out a laugh. "Can't say I blame you, John. Sorry for the interrogation there. We don't get a lot of new people around here."

Bear took a sip of his coffee. "I'm not here to cause any trouble. I'll be out of your hair soon enough."

"That's good. We're not a fan of trouble around here." Sheriff Daniels held up a single finger. "The usual, Doris. Thank you, sweetheart."

"Coffee's good," Bear said, hoping to keep the topic to more neutral ground.

"That it is." Sheriff Daniels waited until Doris poured him a cup before he turned back to Bear. "You know, for the life of me, I could've sworn I'd seen your face somewhere. But it's just not coming to me."

"Really? Maybe I've got a long-lost brother around here somewhere."

Sheriff Daniels chuckled and took a sip of his coffee. "Maybe. They say everyone has a twin, you know. Somewhere in the world."

Bear raised his cup to the idea but didn't speak.

"Where did you say you were heading?" The sheriff clicked his tongue. "There I go again, interrogating you. Sorry about that. Habit of the profession."

"He said he's heading south," Doris said. "But didn't have a destination in mind."

Bear shrugged. "I like driving. Figured the right destination will find me, you know."

"The only people I've ever heard say that have been runnin' from something."

"Life hasn't been too kind to me," Bear said, finishing his coffee. "But I'd say I'm running toward something more than I'm running away from it."

"And what's that?" Doris asked. He had her undivided attention.

Bear wasn't sure what to say. He was just answering questions to keep them off his back, but there was some truth in his words. He might've been running away from the cops, the government, and Hughes in particular, but he was also searching for...something.

"Not sure," he finally answered. "But maybe I'll send a letter back when I figure it out."

Doris beamed just as the cook rang the bell and put the sheriff's food out. She grabbed the plate and set it down in front of Daniels. "The usual, just how you like it, sheriff."

"Thanks, darlin'."

That was Bear's cue. He threw a ten-dollar bill on the counter. "It was nice talking to you both, but I've got to hit the road. Have a good day."

"You, too, Jim," Sheriff Daniels said.

"John," Bear corrected.

"Right. Sorry, I'm so bad at names."

"Stay safe out there," Bear said.

Sheriff Daniels nodded, and while his answers were smooth, Bear could tell the man didn't like the predicament he was in. He couldn't abandon his food and follow Bear, but it was obvious he didn't quite trust Bear was who he said he was, either.

But Bear didn't care. He left the diner and took a sharp left, heading in the opposite direction of the truck. He'd been gone for a good forty-five minutes now. Cara was bound to be worried, but he had to be careful. The last thing he wanted to do was lead the cops back to her.

Instead, Bear took the long way back to the other end of town. He cut down a couple side streets and walked past a few houses, pretending to admire their Fall decorations while keeping his head on a swivel.

It didn't take long to catch sight of the deputy trailing him in his car.

Every time Bear turned onto a new street, he saw the officer turn down the road he'd just stepped off of. The deputy would've been better off leaving the car behind and following him on foot, but considering Bear's size and the fact that he was a complete unknown, it seemed the sheriff's department was not taking any risks.

Bear wondered if they had any inkling of who he was, or if they really just didn't get that many new people around these parts. Maybe this was their way of entertaining themselves on a random Tuesday morning.

Either way, it was a pain in Bear's ass. He had to lose his tail—and fast.

Bear made his way back to the main road, crossed it, and ended up on the east side of town. It didn't look much different from the west side, but it did put more distance between him and the deputy following him. He'd almost made it to the edge of town when the deputy car cut him off at the corner, right outside a bar. It wasn't even noon yet, but it was already open. A couple old-timers sat inside.

The deputy hadn't turned on his lights or his siren, so nobody took notice of the vehicle. Bear took a couple steps back, positioning himself at the corner of the alley. He waited until the officer got out of his car and made his way over to him.

He was a tall, thin man with a hooked nose and a large fore-head. Bear immediately disliked him.

"Morning, sir," Bear said. "What can I do for you?"

"I need you to turn and face the wall. Lock your hands behind your head and spread your legs."

Bear let confusion color his face. "Can I ask what this is about, officer?"

The deputy put his hand on his weapon and unbuttoned the holster, but didn't remove the gun. "Turn and face the wall. Now."

Bear complied, locking his hands and spreading his legs.

The deputy walked up to him and proceeded to pat him down. "We got a couple calls of a man casing the neighborhood."

"I wasn't casing the neighborhood. I was going for a walk."

"Sheriff said you hurried out of the diner to get back on the road."

"I got turned around," Bear said. "I've never been here before. Forgot which direction I'd parked in. Figured looking at the houses while I was at it wouldn't be a crime against humanity."

"Don't get smart," the deputy said.

"I could act dumb if you want me to," Bear said.

He couldn't help it. Sometimes the sarcasm just couldn't be controlled.

The deputy grabbed one of Bear's arms and yanked it behind his back. "Resisting arrest? I'll have to cuff you for that."

Bear didn't bother arguing with him. He knew the second the deputy got out of his car that this wasn't going to end well. Instead of waiting for the other man to get the handcuffs around one of his wrists, Bear threw an elbow and connected with the man's nose. When he twisted around to see the damage he'd done, Bear was happy to find blood gushing from the middle of the deputy's face.

"*Now* I'm resisting arrest," Bear said.

As the deputy reached for his gun, Bear grabbed his wrist and twisted. The other man was no match for Bear's strength and immediately cried out in pain. One quick punch to the temple got him to shut up. His eyes fluttered shut. The handcuffs fell to the ground.

Bear didn't waste any time. He grabbed the cuffs and dragged the deputy to the alley, where he cuffed him to the dumpster and yanked the radio from his shirt, tossing it into the garbage. As the deputy came to, Bear knelt down in front of him.

"You just had to go and be a dick," Bear said. "You could've let me walk out of this town without causing any trouble, but you had something to prove, didn't you?"

The deputy sputtered but couldn't find his words.

"Guess you proved it now. Good luck explaining this one to your sheriff."

Bear knew he'd only had a few minutes head start. As soon as the deputy didn't answer his radio, someone would go looking for him. Probably the sheriff.

Bear planned on being far away from New Glarus by the time that happened.

25

CARA WAS SITTING IN THE FRONT SEAT OF THE TRUCK WITH BOTH hands on the wheel when Bear rounded the corner and made his way over to her. He could see her visibly relax before sliding over and unlocking the doors.

"What took so long?"

"Ran into a little trouble."

She looked him up and down. "Are you okay?"

"I'm fine," Bear said. "The sheriff's deputy, on the other hand, probably has a broken nose. Definitely a bruised ego."

"What did you do?"

Bear threw his hands up. "I didn't start it. The sheriff was on my ass as soon as I got to the post office. Ditched him at the diner and almost made it back before one of his lackeys decided to try something."

"Oh, so you had time to stop for more food?" Cara went from angry to hopeful within the span of a single second. "Did you bring anything for me?"

"All I got was a mediocre cup of coffee. I wasn't sticking around for the specials."

Cara *harrumphed* and repositioned her seat without another word.

"Did anyone pass by here?"

"You told me to keep my head down."

Bear leveled a stare at her. "Did you *hear* anyone?"

"A couple cars," she relented.

"Were they heading into town or out of it?"

"Into it. Why?"

Bear put the car in drive and eased his way onto the road. "If they were heading out, it could've been one of the sheriff's deputies who could've circled back around. It means we've got a little longer before we have to give up the truck. Either way, we should switch cars sooner rather than later."

The cab of the Silverado was filled with silence for the next few miles. Cara stared out the window while Bear kept an eye on the rearview mirror. There were no cars following them, least of all a patrol vehicle. By this time, the sheriff probably found his deputy. They might send someone out to look for Bear, but he'd be long gone by then.

Cara broke the silence first. "Thank you, by the way."

"For what?"

"For doing that." She fluttered her hands around. "For all of it. For everything."

"You don't have to thank me."

She laughed. "I kind of do. You saved my life, more than once. I know you'd be a lot better off without me. So, just accept my thanks, okay? Please?"

Bear's tongue was heavy. "You're welcome."

"I think—" Cara's voice cut out and she cleared her throat

before she started again. "I think I should tell you who my contact is now."

"Oh?" Every nerve in Bear's body was tuned into the words coming out of Cara's mouth. "Why now?"

"Didn't you hear the part where I finally recognized that I owe you my life? We're in this together. You need to know. Maybe you can help me."

"Help with what?"

"Getting into contact with him."

"I thought that's what the editorial was for."

"It is." Cara twisted her hands in her lap. "That's the signal, but I still need to make contact. We have a backup plan for when he knows I'm ready to talk. I just need to get to a computer. The rest will work itself out."

"For the record," Bear said, "no plan that ends with *the rest will work itself out* is ever a good plan."

"Like you've never winged it before."

Bear had to give her that one. "I avoid winging it whenever possible."

Then, out of nowhere: "It's the Vice President."

Bear felt that *zing* throughout his nerves again. "The Vice President of the United States?"

Cara's voice was slow and muted, and Bear couldn't tell if it was because she was having trouble getting it out or if he was having trouble processing it.

"The Vice President of the United States."

It took all of Bear's self-control not to immediately slam on the breaks. Instead, he triple-checked the mirror and then fixed his eyes on the road ahead before he answered.

"You mean to tell me," he managed to get out, "your contact, your informant, is the Vice President. Of the United States. Of America."

"Yes."

Bear looked at Cara out of the corner of his eye. "You're gonna have to help me with this one."

Cara sighed and tipped her head back. "When I first started gathering information for the story, I didn't know how big it was. Had no fucking clue what I was getting into. I was poking my nose where it didn't belong, and some people started to take notice. When you start throwing around words like *conspiracy* and *corruption*, government officials get a little antsy."

"Fair enough."

"I got an anonymous message warning me to be careful. At first, I thought it was a threat. I ignored it. Kept digging. The messages came every night. I started taking them more seriously. Then, one day, they dropped some information in my lap."

"That seems convenient."

Cara ignored him. "They pointed me in the direction of Mateo. I'd heard of him before that, obviously, but I didn't know he was connected in any way. I started digging deeper. I was careful this time. Quieter. I found out how he had been connected to Goddard's pipeline expansion, how he had opposed it. He had used it as an excuse to meet with politicians in D.C., but he ended up sticking around."

Bear's voice was slow as he worked through his memories of the last day or so. "When Goldstone mentioned Hughes and Mateo had met with the Vice President, you didn't even blink."

Cara shrugged, but she looked proud of herself. "I already knew about the meeting. It didn't shock me that it had come up in the records."

Bear made a mental note not to play Cara in a game of poker. "This person messaging you could've been anybody."

"That's what I thought, too. I took it with a grain of salt. What they were telling me was lining up, but I still had to confirm who it was. Obviously, he wasn't keen on revealing his identity. So, I asked to meet in person. On his terms. No cameras, no recording devices. He needed me to blow this story wide open and I needed him to feed me the right information."

"Hold up," Bear said, putting a hand out. "Why was he so interested in what Hughes was doing in the first place."

"Human decency? Patriotism?"

"He probably wants something out of it," Bear said.

"You're probably right. I'm sure there's a lot to gain from revealing a conspiracy and corruption that has infected the top positions of the White House. Adams is still pretty young. He's got a good base. He'll probably try for a presidential bid after this."

"So, maybe it's not altruism," Bear said. "It's about taking out the contenders. Hughes would be a big threat to his presidential campaign if his plan went through."

"It might not be altruism, but he's still doing the right thing."

"I still don't like it." Bear shifted lanes on the highway and checked the rearview mirror again. "He's using a young reporter to gather evidence to corroborate the story instead of going through official channels."

"Can you blame him?" Cara ran a hand through her hair. "He's got to stay far away from this until we're ready to go public. Hughes is the director of National Intelligence. He has the resources to bury anyone, even the Vice President."

Bear couldn't argue with that. "So, you asked to meet your informant in person. With no backup or proof of the meeting. You realize you could've been walking into a trap, right?"

"I had a taser."

Bear shot her a look. "Not helping."

"I know it was dumb," Cara said, "but I was desperate. My story was a lot of loose ends. I needed someone who would be willing to go on record to confirm everything I had found, to link everything together and point it at Hughes."

Bear had a lot of questions, but they'd have to wait. "So, what happened?"

"He gave me a time and a place. I showed up. He was alone. It was a bit of a shock to come face to face with the Vice President. Lost my voice there for a minute. He was nice, though. Very secretive. He made me take off my jacket, empty out my purse and pockets. Said I was smart for bringing the taser."

"And then handed you all the information you needed?"

"No." Cara laughed. "He said he couldn't risk giving me any details of the meetings he'd been in. They'd know the information was coming from him. He just gave me a nudge in the right direction. I had to put the pieces together. When I was ready, he'd step forward. We'd do it together."

"So, why doesn't he bring us in? Protect us?"

"He doesn't know who he can trust. Hughes is the *Director of National Intelligence*. There's no telling who he's got in his pocket."

"Fair enough." Bear scratched his chin. "So, what's the next step?"

"We wait until my story is printed. Adams will know that means it's time to get into contact with me. By now he's realized my phone is gone. That means we'll have to connect on a secure server he set up for us. We're the only ones who can access it. We'll decide where to go from there."

Bear wished he could see beyond just the next step in their plan, but this would have to do for now. Having the Vice President on your side sounded like just about the biggest win you could get, but he wasn't convinced Adams would have the balls to step up to the plate. They'd have to catch Hughes with a smoking gun in his hand if they wanted to pin all of this on him. Anything less than that, and Bear was sure Adams would find some excuse to get cold feet."

"So," Cara said, interrupting his thoughts, "where to next?"

"The closer, the better," Bear said. He spotted an upcoming exit that would stop taking them south and start taking them east.

"What's that mean?"

"It means it's time we head to D.C."

26

BEAR SET THEIR NEW DESTINATION AS FAIRFAX, VIRGINIA. IT WAS less than an hour outside D.C., and even though it was about ten times bigger than good ol' New Glarus, Bear wasn't too worried about being spotted, as long as they were smart. The fact that Cara could pass for a college student didn't hurt, either.

Bear drove until it was dark, then look a random exit and looked for the cheapest motel he could find. This one required a credit card, so he handed Cara one with a fake name and sent her on her way. Bear couldn't tell if he was proud or concerned that she was getting better at going with the flow now. She got the room without any resistance, and even remembered to ask for one on the ground floor and near an exit.

They didn't talk much that night. There wasn't a whole lot to be said, anyway. They had their new heading and the beginnings of a rudimentary plan to get them out of this hole they had both found themselves in. For now, that would be enough.

Besides, long drives always seemed to take their toll, even if you were just sitting there all day. Something about the monotony of the road sucked all the energy from your bones. The two of them traded off showers and then hit their beds without so much as a goodnight.

The following morning, Bear woke up at the crack of dawn, ready to get rolling. Cara took a little longer to come around, but she managed to walk to the truck on her own before passing out again. Bear risked grabbing them both coffee, and soon enough, they were back on the road.

Several hours later, Bear pulled to a stop, jolting Cara awake from her second nap of the day. She glared at him while he grinned and shrugged. He'd take his entertainment where he could get it.

"What's the plan?" She stretched and Bear heard a couple joints pop.

"We need a computer."

"Library?"

"I thought about that, too, but I don't like the idea of being cooped up in a building like that. I'd rather have full view of the street and an easy escape route."

"Where else are we going to get free computer time?"

"We're not." Bear reached into his wallet and pulled out a different credit card. "We'll need to buy a laptop. Something cheap. We just need it for the internet."

"Must be nice to have money to throw away on a computer we'll only use once." Cara took the card and looked at it. "You don't look like a Mr. Alex Monroe."

All Bear said was, "Looks can be deceiving."

Bear sent Cara off down Main Street to find a store that sold computers and buy the cheapest one available. Her story would be that her computer crashed and she needed something to finish her paper for school. The card was her father's. If they needed proof, she'd have them call Bear.

It didn't come to that. Twenty minutes later, Cara walked up to the truck with a grin on her face and a bag under her arm.

"Success," she said, as soon as she slid back into her seat. "Only cost you $600."

"Only." Bear rolled his eyes. "They didn't have anything cheaper?"

"This was the best I could do." She handed back his card. "What's step two?"

"Find a café with Wi-Fi."

"That shouldn't be hard. There's about twelve dozen of them down there."

"We need one with a back entrance."

Cara pinched her eyebrows together. "That's a bit more specific."

"It's always good to have a backup plan."

She shrugged. "You're the expert."

Bear took in the area around him, and when he was sure no one was watching too closely, he slid out of the truck and made his way toward Main Street. He had instructed Cara to wait for a count of sixty before following him. She needed to keep an eye on him without walking too close. Bear didn't want anyone seeing them enter the café together. Once inside, they'd have to risk sitting at the same table. He wanted to keep an eye on everything Vice President Adams was saying.

Bear walked the length of Main Street and then back up the other side. Halfway down, he spotted a café with a little alley along the side. A door set in the brick wall told him they'd have an exit strategy that didn't involve busting out through the front door. It was better than nothing.

The café was small and dark—perfect for them. Bear took a seat in the far corner and waited for Cara to show up. He counted to sixty. And then sixty again. His mind started to spiral. What if

Hughes was already one step ahead of them? What if Cara had been taken in broad daylight right from the sidewalk. What if—

The doorbell chimed and she walked through the door. Her face was flushed. She made a beeline for Bear's table and slid into the seat next to him.

"Hey," he said, by way of keeping up appearances.

"Hi!" She overdid it on the cheer. Then, under her breath, "You walk so fast."

He refused to admit to her that she'd had him worried for a second. Better not let it go to her head. Instead, he slipped her a ten and had her order them a coffee and a couple muffins. He unwrapped the computer, but let her set it up. He wanted to focus on everything around them.

The café was quiet for being a morning in the middle of the week. Only a couple other patrons sat there sipping their coffee or eating their breakfast. One young woman had a book balanced precariously on her lap while she tried to eat a doughnut. There was powdered sugar all over her pants.

An older man sat reading a newspaper, sipping slowly but steadily from his mug. He looked like he could be a professor. Next to him was a young man with headphones in. He was tapping away at his computer with the kind of fervor Bear imagined only belonged to a college student on a deadline.

Outside the window, people passed to and fro. Once in a while, someone would stop in, order a coffee, and then leave.

"Got it," Cara said. She slid the computer over so they could both see the screen.

"Now what?"

"Now we get the ball rolling."

It was interesting to see the transformation in the young reporter. Bear had seen a confidence and resolve from her since the beginning, but now Cara was in her element. She typed in a website from memory and entered a username and password. It required a second and third form of verification, but her fingers danced over the keyboard so quickly, Bear wouldn't have been able to see what she was doing if he tried.

After a couple minutes, Cara sat back with a sigh of relief and gestured toward the computer. "There you go."

Bear leaned forward. "It's a blank page. With a blinking cursor."

"It's a very important blank page," Cara corrected, "with a very important blinking cursor."

"What do we do next?"

"We wait." Cara took a sip from her coffee. "He'll have gotten a notification I logged on. He'll get on as soon as he can so we can figure out where to go from here, but it could take some time. He'll need to find somewhere secure where no one will be able to see what he's doing."

"Makes you wonder if the Capitol is the worst place for that sort of thing—or the best."

Cara nodded and bit into her muffin. "My guess is the best. If you-know-who got as far as he did, then we should be just fine."

"Famous last words," Bear said.

27

TURNED OUT BEAR WASN'T TOO FAR OFF FROM THE TRUTH.

It had been a solid two hours before something happened, but it wasn't exactly what Cara had been expecting. While the page had remained blank, the sidewalk outside the café picked up in activity.

To the average person, nothing would have seemed out of the ordinary. Just like two hours prior, people were walking up and down the sidewalk, sometimes coming in for a cup of coffee, sometimes sitting on the bench outside to talk with their friends.

Bear, however, caught two different people walk by twice, looking into the café and then moving on. If it were a college student or even someone who looked like the old professor who'd left an hour ago, he wouldn't have paid much mind. Despite their innocuous outside appearances, Bear could tell they were military men. Someone had hired them to keep an eye on him and Cara.

The final straw came when a middle-aged man entered the café and ordered a small cup of coffee. He took it and sat down a couple tables away. He wasn't nervous, but he was stiff and practiced in his movements. He never touched his coffee. He had his phone out, but he clearly wasn't reading whatever article he had pulled up to make himself look busy.

Bear leaned close to Cara under the premise of getting a better look at the screen. "We've got company."

She froze. She had clearly picked up enough from Bear because she didn't bother looking over to see what was going on beyond the scope of their own little table. "Who is it?"

"Not sure. Probably Hughes' men, but that's just a guess."

"A good guess."

"We need to leave everything and run."

Cara's fingers gripped the edges of the computer. "We can't. This is our chance, Bear. We can't risk losing it. It could be days before we get a setup like this again."

Bear knew she was right, but he still didn't like the idea of lugging around a computer connected to a private server that linked them to the Vice President of the United States. There were a lot of ways this could go wrong. And it looked like it already had.

"Pack up your bag, leave the computer." Bear held up a hand when Cara started to protest. "Ask where the bathroom is. Don't be quiet about it. There should be a side door that leads to the alley. Meet me out there. I'll follow you in a minute. I'll bring the computer."

Cara looked from the computer to Bear as if she didn't trust him to follow through on his word, but what other choice did they have? She threw the remnants of the computer's packaging into the bag and slid out from behind the table.

Bear noticed the man two tables down had stopped scrolling on his phone.

Cara loudly asked where the bathroom was and headed to the back of the café without hesitation. Bear didn't like having her out of sight, but they didn't have much choice. He needed to keep an eye on their new friend and anyone else at the front of the café who might cause trouble.

The man two tables down started typing on his phone. That was Bear's cue. Whoever this guy was with, he was alerting them to Cara's movements. If they had any suspicion that the two of them would make a break for it, that meant someone would be waiting for them out back.

But taking on one or two people in an alleyway was much smarter than taking on several more along Main Street.

Bear snapped the computer shut, tucked it under his arm, and made a beeline for the bathrooms. The door to the alley was marked as an exit. He didn't bother being quiet about opening it. The man in the café would know they were plotting their escape either way.

As soon as Bear had one foot out the door, he could feel the tension in the air. Another step put him out into the alley. A third and final step allowed the door to swing shut behind him.

A man with a gun had his sights set on Cara, who was on her knees with her hands behind her head. Even from his vantage point, Bear could see her shaking. A single tear rolled down her cheek.

As soon as Bear emerged from the café, the man switched his attention to the bigger threat.

Bear got a good look at the man behind the gun. His hair was sandy and he had the slightest emergence of a blond mustache growing above his lip. He looked a little squirrely, a little jittery. He also looked young. Bear tried to weigh whether that would be to his advantage or not. On the one hand, it could make the man an easier target. On the other, it could make him extra jumpy. If it was the latter, he was bound to do something stupid.

"On the ground!"

Bear held up his hands, the one still carrying the laptop. He saw the man's eyes flick to it for the briefest of seconds. Bear took a single step forward.

"I said *on the ground!*"

"Okay, pal. Calm down." Bear took another step forward. He saw the man's finger twitch. "I just want to make sure the girl is okay."

"She's fine," he spat out. "On the ground. Now."

"Sure thing." Bear risked taking one more step forward. He was now lined up with Cara and only about a foot and a half away from the man who held them at gunpoint. The rookie was too close, and Bear was more than ready to use that to their advantage.

Bear started to kneel, putting one knee on the asphalt but leaving the other one under him. He flipped the computer so the screen was facing down and gripped it with both hands. "I'm just going to lay this on the ground first, okay?"

The man's finger twitched again. "Hurry up."

Bear could see beads of sweat rolling down the man's face. He wondered what he'd been told about Bear. Was he considered armed and extremely dangerous? Did he believe Bear had killed Mateo, and maybe others? Was he being fed misinformation that was much worse?

Bear wanted to ask the rookie who he worked for, but he had a gut feeling that any further conversation would get him an accidental bullet in the shoulder. Or somewhere worse. So, instead, he took a deep breath and acted.

Instead of dropping his other knee to the ground, Bear surged upward, bringing the computer around to smack the gun out of the man's hand. It went off, but the bullet went wide. The gun skittered down the alley and out of range.

The rookie's eyes went wide. He was already pale, but Bear saw the blood drain from his face, turning him into a ghost. The man's hands immediately shot up.

"Please don't kill me."

"Whatever they told you about me, they're wrong," Bear said.

The rookie was a withering mess.

"But I do have to apologize."

The man managed to get two words out. "For what?"

"This is going to hurt."

Bear cocked his arm back and threw it forward. His fist connected with the rookie's temple and sent his body crumpling to the ground. He'd wake up with a sizeable bruise and a killer headache, but all things considered, he was getting off easy.

The rookie wouldn't be out for long, so Bear didn't waste any time. He turned back to Cara, who was still kneeling on the ground.

"Get up," he said, handing her the computer. "We need to go."

Cara scrambled to her feet. "Go where? Who was that?"

"I'm going to figure that out along the way."

Bear didn't bother making sure Cara was following. By now, she knew she had to keep up or risk getting left behind. They only had seconds to lose their tails. Every move they made had to be calculated a hundred different ways.

But this was what Bear lived for. This was what he was good at.

The pair ran away toward the other end of the alley and away from Main Street. Bear rounded the corner, half expecting an entire fleet of police cars to greet them. There was no one. Maybe the people after them hadn't been informed as to who he really was. If they had, there'd be a lot more manpower on the street right now.

Their mistake.

Bear took off down the street, not bothering to blend in. They needed to get as far away from the café as possible. He had to assume the truck was compromised. They'd need another car as their getaway vehicle.

Luckily, they were in a college town with plenty of clunkers that would blend right into the everyday grind.

They were at least five blocks away by the time Bear had slowed to a walk. Cara was half a block behind him but keeping pace. Her face was flushed and she was breathing heavy, but she didn't complain. It was either run or end up in a jail cell. Or worse.

Not great odds.

Bear's eyes were roaming left and right, looking for the perfect car.

Cara held a stitch in her side. "What's the next move?"

Bear didn't answer right away. He waited until his eyes landed on what he was looking for.

It was a 1997 Honda Accord. Silver, with a busted side mirror and a dent in the bumper. Perfect.

"I'm tired of running," Bear said. He made a beeline for the car. "We're gonna bring the fight to them."

28

"BEAR?"

"Yeah?"

"It's working."

Bear slid closer to the computer to get a better look at it. There was a single message at the top. It just read *I don't have much time.*

Bear leaned back. "Good. Neither do we."

He had driven them directly to Washington D.C. They stopped at the first café they found, ordered a coffee, and opened up the computer. They had waited half an hour before moving on. They walked a couple blocks, got another coffee, and repeated the process.

This was the fourth café they had stopped at and the first time Adams had been online.

"He's asking how I am, what's been going on."

Bear kept his eyes out the windows and not on the computer. "We don't have time for that. We need to know what the plan is."

Cara tapped away at the keyboard. Bear trusted her to relay the message.

"He wants to meet up." She hit a few more keys. "Tomorrow. He wants to talk face-to-face."

"I still don't like it."

Cara looked up and Bear met her eyes. She looked scared and determined all at once. "Do we have another choice?"

"We have a lot of choices," Bear said. "But this one will get us the biggest results."

"At the highest risk."

Bear grinned. "Now you're learning."

"Constitution Gardens. Tomorrow. Noon. He'll have a contact meet us. Someone he trusts."

Bear shook his head. "That's no good. I don't trust *him* let alone whoever *he* trusts."

"He's the Vice President of the United States." Cara's voice was so quiet, Bear had to lean forward to hear her. "He's not going to meet us out in the open like that."

Bear's phone vibrated in his pocket. He took it out and smiled at the number that popped up. "Fine, but I'm going to have a backup plan."

"I'd expect nothing less."

While Cara went back to the computer, Bear flipped his phone open. He kept his voice even, but his heart was pounding. "Got anything good for me?"

Brandon's voice filled Bear's ear. "Yes and no."

"Hit me with it."

"Hughes is currently in D.C. As far as I can tell, he's not planning on going anywhere. His official schedule has him locked up in meetings all week. He goes home to his wife every night. Visits with his grandkids on the weekend when he can."

"I feel a *but* coming along."

"*But*," Brandon emphasized, "he's been making a lot of phone calls. Talking to a bunch of interesting people."

"Like who?"

Brandon sighed. "Look, I know you know this, but I have to just say it out loud. I had to pull in a lot of favors for this. Like, top tier favors that I probably won't ever have again."

"I appreciate that." Bear kept his voice measured. "You know the stakes here."

"I do." Brandon sighed again. "I do, and it's going to be worth it if we can nail this guy to the wall. I'm just saying—I've tapped the well for a while, okay?"

"I understand. I appreciate it. Anything you need, you let me or Jack know, okay? Anything."

The sound of typing filled the other end of the phone. "So, these phone calls."

"Who's he been talking to?"

"A lot of people." More typing. "Ex-military. The kind the military doesn't admit to having employed. Snipers, mostly. They're not good guys. Pair of brothers. Their names are Craig and Sean O'Reilly. From what I can tell, you only hire them when you've got one shot to take out a target."

Bear's eyes slid to Cara. "Any idea who they've got their eye on?"

"Couldn't find anything. They're old school. Like to meet in person, keep physical logs. They're quick, clean, and meticulous. Do you think they're coming after you?"

"Maybe." But Bear had his doubts. "What else is going on?"

There were a few more keystrokes before Brandon answered. "A lot of people in D.C. respect Hughes, but they don't necessarily like him. They think he gets the job done, but some of them are worried about the price it costs."

"I suspected as much." Bear looked at the clock on Cara's computer. They were running out of time. "Any details I can use?"

"Maybe." Brandon paused in his typing. "I have one person, a low-level guy, claims he found some incriminating evidence against Hughes. He sent it to me right before he disappeared."

Bear sat up straighter. "Disappeared?"

"I can't find him. Maybe he went off the grid. Maybe they found out."

There was a chance they'd never find out which it was, and Bear had a feeling Brandon already knew that. "What did he send you?"

A few more clicks. "My buddy tapped his phone. I don't know how he managed it, but I have two clear recordings of Hughes talking to someone about a possible attack."

Bear lowered his voice. "He is the Director of National Intelligence. That's his job. I'm going to need something more—"

"I mean," Brandon interrupted, "they're talking about hiring a group of insurgents to plan an attack. They're arguing about the best possible place to do it. In the two recordings I have, they don't say where, but they list a few options."

Bear glanced at the clock again. Time was up. "Any idea who the other guy is?"

"I couldn't pinpoint who it was." The frustration was evident in Brandon's voice. "The phone distorts it, so running comparative analysis is proving...difficult."

"Keep working that angle. Send it to Jack. This might be exactly what we need to blow this thing wide open."

"I know you've been in a lot of sticky situations before," Brandon said, "but this one feels different. Bigger. These guys are smart. Calculated. The way they were talking about killing thousands of innocent people..."

"I'll be careful," Bear said. "And we'll be smart."

"See that you do."

"Thanks, man. I mean it. I know you stuck your neck out for me. For all of us."

"Just do me a favor and take this guy down."

"That's the plan."

Bear hung up the phone and turned to Cara. "We've got to go."

"We're all set here." She disconnected from the server and closed the lid.

Bear stood and made his way to the front of the store. Cara followed him after executing a command to wipe the laptop hard drive. They left the laptop behind. One of Hughes' men would probably interrogate the barista who would end up finding it, but it didn't matter. He and Cara would be in the wind.

"We've got to find a new car, don't we?" Cara asked.

"You are a quick learner." Bear headed away from the busy street they were on, his eyes constantly on the lookout for some beat up old car that would blend into the crowd. "But there's something else we have to discuss first."

"Your conversation with whoever was on the phone. It sounded serious."

Bear didn't know how else to break the news to her, so he just said it. "This meeting is going to be dangerous. There's reason to believe we're not going to be the only ones in attendance."

Cara looked up at him. "What's that supposed to mean?"

"A pair of brothers. Snipers. They might be on the lookout for us."

"Might be?"

Bear shrugged. "There's a good chance."

"You don't want me to go, do you?"

"Not if I can help it."

Cara ran a hand through her hair. She found a knot and worked her way through it. "You know I have to be there. Adams' contact isn't going to talk to anyone but me."

"We just need to give ourselves enough time to find the snipers and take them out."

"So, what? We get a body double?"

Bear stopped and turned to Cara. He looked her up and down, a grin forming across his face.

"Yeah. And I've got the perfect person."

29

BEAR APPROACHED THE STORAGE FACILITY WITH CAUTION. IT WAS IN a self-accessible warehouse, which meant there was no telling who was inside. If you had the keycode, you could get in. If anyone had gotten wind that he'd be there today, they could be lying in wait.

He held out his arm to stop Cara from walking forward. She looked up at him, her pupils dilated with fear. She was doing better at keeping it together despite their situation, but it took years of training for logic to outweigh an emotional response. She wasn't quite there just yet.

Bear punched in the five-digit keycode he'd been given. The door buzzed and released. He put his hand on the knob and pulled it open slowly. His gun was tucked out of sight, and he didn't want to bring it out unless necessary. Better to lay low in case there were any civilians around.

Cara followed him through the door and let it click shut behind them. An electronic buzzing indicated it was once again locked. The young reporter jumped at the noise and then exhaled loudly. Bear heard her mutter a couple curse words under her breath.

"Quickly but quietly," Bear said.

Cara nodded.

He led them down the length of the building, heading for the final row on the far side. The storage units were larger here. They could house multiple cars or an entire three-story house full of furniture. They didn't come cheap. But they did offer plenty of privacy.

The hallways were clean, the walls sterile. Bear felt trapped by the building. The innumerable rows of units were oppressive. The bright fluorescent lights were harsh, but the lack of shadows in any corner of the building offered a modicum of comfort.

Halfway down the row, Bear stopped and Cara came to a halt behind him. Unit 2552. It looked like all the others, but inside offered them the solution to their current problem. Or so he hoped.

The door to the unit was painted bright red, like all the others. It lifted like a garage door. It looked sturdy enough, but not bullet proof. Normally, that wasn't a deal breaker for the kind of people who were looking for the services offered here.

For Bear, it almost made him turn around and walk the other way.

These doors weren't on an electronic system like the front. Instead, they were attached with a physical lock to the ground by a bolt in the cement. This one had already been opened. The lock was missing and the latch was flipped open. Someone was already inside.

He knocked twice, waited a count of ten, and then knocked two more times.

The door began to lift. Despite its size and heft, it was quiet as it rolled up, first revealing a pair of black boots, then dark jeans, a plain shirt and bomber jacket, and finally the face of the one person who could pull off doubling for Cara.

"Hello, Riley."

"Hello, Sadie." Bear couldn't help but grin. It was nice to see her again. "How're you doing?"

"Not bad." Her eyes shifted to Cara. "You must be Ms. Bishop."

Cara stuck out her hand. "Cara is fine."

"My name is Sadie. Come on in."

Bear ducked through the opening with Cara right on his heels. He watched as Sadie dropped the door back down before looking at the space they were working in. It wasn't much, just an open area with a couple tables in the center. A pair of construction lights managed to illuminate the unit, but nothing nearly as bright as what was outside. It took Bear a minute for his eyes to adjust.

"Get here okay?" Sadie asked.

"Yeah." Bear pulled out a chair and sat down heavily. "We stayed in a motel outside of the city."

"Accommodations okay?"

"I've had worse."

Cara snorted. "Seriously?"

Sadie smiled. "Do I need to apologize on his behalf? Bear can be a little gruff sometimes."

Cara looked at Bear, and he could've sworn there was a softness in her eyes. "We got off to a rocky start, but I think we're doing okay now." She turned serious. "I don't think I'll ever be able to repay him—either of you—for what you've done for me."

Bear held up a hand. "Don't mention it."

"Seriously, don't mention it." There was a twinkle in Sadie's eye. "Bear gets uncomfortable if we emote too much."

"Ha, ha." Bear tried to scowl, but he couldn't help his grin. "You been good? Anyone give you any trouble recently?"

She shrugged. "Nothing I couldn't handle. Couple people have been nosing around. As soon as your face popped up on the news, I knew someone would come around. Couple guys tried to get me to tell them where you were. I said I had no idea. We hadn't been in contact. I had nothing to hide and there was nothing to find."

"We both know having nothing to hide doesn't mean they wouldn't find something to keep you detained."

She shrugged. "I've kept my head down since the last time I saw you. I've been diligent. Work and sleep, that's all I've been doing. Sitting behind a desk hasn't been ideal, but it's kept me close to the paper trail. I've picked up a couple things here and there, quietly. There's been inquiries, but they know where I am every day. They can keep an eye on me. They started looking elsewhere."

"And now?" Bear asked, motioning to the unit around them. "They're gonna wonder where you went."

"Let me worry about that." Sadie put a hand on Bear's shoulder. "If we do this right, if we get it done quickly, they won't have time to know I'm missing."

"Did you find anything else out about the O'Reilly brothers?"

Sadie grabbed a folder from the table and handed it to Bear. "Nothing good. These guys are the best. And I mean that literally. I've never seen a track record as good as this. They work as a pair, so there's always a contingency plan. They don't miss, Bear. Not ever."

"We've had worse odds before."

"I haven't." Cara's voice was quiet. "This is insane. You know that, right?"

Sadie's face softened. "You're going to be far away from here when this goes down."

"But you won't be." There were tears in her eyes now. "You could die."

"I know this probably sounds crazy to you, but that's part of the job. We knew what we were signing up for." Sadie gestured to Bear. "There's only two people on this entire planet I would trust to keep me safe, and one of them is sitting right there."

Bear flipped through the file he had been given. "Even so, with two shooters, we're gonna need backup. There's no way we can trace and take them both down."

"I've got someone in mind."

Bear shook his head. "Who is it? Not another spook. We can't trust anyone. There's nothing indicating who Hughes has in his pocket."

"This guy's got a good track record." Sadie was interrupted by a double knock. Everyone in the room froze. Ten seconds later, there was another double knock. "And it seems like he's arrived a little early."

Bear stood up and placed himself between Cara and the door. Sadie walked up to the sliding partition and grabbed the handle at the bottom. When she lifted it up, the room was flooded with fluorescent light. Bear had to blink a few times before he could see. He instinctively reached for the weapon tucked against the small of his back.

The voice of the newcomer was immediately familiar. "Hey, big man. Miss me?"

30

Bear immediately felt relief wash over him. Jack entered the storage unit as Sadie lowered the door behind him. Bear shook his head at his old friend.

"How did you get back into the States?"

Jack hooked a thumb over his shoulder at Sadie. "A lot of coordination and a couple trips in the back of a very sketchy plane. It was touch-and-go a few times."

"It was never touch-and-go." Sadie smacked Jack's arm. "It was a smooth ride from start to finish. Stop being dramatic."

Jack grinned and shrugged. His eyes landed on Cara and he extended his hand. "It's nice to finally meet you face-to-face. I'm sorry you're mixed up in all of this.

Cara shook his hand, and Bear caught something akin to awe in her face before she reined it in. "It's nice to finally meet you, too. Thank you—for everything."

"Don't thank me yet." Jack made his way over to the tables in the center of the room. "We have a lot to work out first."

Bear joined him. "What do you know so far?"

"He's up to speed, except for the O'Reilly brothers." Sadie handed Jack the file Bear had been reading. "I was just filling Bear in on what we're up against."

"I've heard of these guys," Jack said, flipping through the pages. "They're good."

"It's been said once or twice." Bear shot a look to Sadie. "But we'll have to be better."

The four of them gathered around the table. Sadie took the lead. "The meeting is set up in Constitution Gardens. Noon. We don't have an exact location yet, which is probably for the best. They won't know where we'll be headed."

"But that also means we won't know where they'll be pointing their guns in order to trace it back to their location," Jack offered.

"That's where you're gonna come in." Sadie rolled out a map of the park. "They were smart when they set up the meeting. If they're going to hole up in a building, it'll be along Constitution Ave. Even if we come up from the south, where the Lincoln Memorial Reflecting Pool is located, we'll have to circle north and put our backs to the street to get to the island in the middle of the pond."

"He never said meet at the pond," Cara offered.

Sadie's smile was gentle. "No, but if I were setting up a hit, that's where I would want it. One way in, one way out. Even if we're forced into the water, it'll give them time to circle around and meet us on the bank at the other side."

"We need to take out the snipers before you ever even get to the island," Jack said.

"The O'Reilly brothers will have Bear and Cara's pictures, probably the ones from the news. They'll spot us the second we get close to the Gardens. It's gonna be up to you to take them out."

Jack rubbed the side of his face. There was some significant stubble there. "They'll be covering as much ground as they can, which means they won't be close together. I'll be able to take one out no problem, but the other one is gonna be harder. Especially if they're checking in periodically. If they get any indication something is going wrong, they'll either bail or take the shot."

"We're meeting at noon and tomorrow is going to be sunny. That'll work in our favor."

Cara's voice was small, like she wasn't sure she should interrupt their conversation. "How?"

"Higher chances of the sun reflecting off the scope of their weapon," Bear said. "But knowing where the bullet is coming from won't stop it."

"Isn't that like looking for a needle in a haystack?" Cara asked.

Jack grinned. "Yes, but we're very good at finding needles in haystacks."

Sadie pointed at the island on the map. "Bear and I will be focused on whoever we're meeting and keeping an eye out for anyone in the park who looks like they don't belong. It'll be up to you to watch our backs, Jack."

Bear didn't like the setup. "Isn't there anyone else we can bring in for this?"

"Like who?" Jack sat down and kicked his feet up on the table. "Most of the people we can trust are in this room, and those who aren't shouldn't have to put their necks on the line for us."

"But it's not just for us," Bear countered. "We're talking about stopping an act of global terrorism."

"With little proof and high chances for it to go sideways. Would you want to throw anyone into those odds?"

Bear didn't want to lose the argument, but he knew Jack was right. "Goldstone says hello, by the way."

Jack grinned. "How is the old man?"

"Still old," Bear said. "Still can kick your ass."

Sadie cleared her throat and waited for the two men to give her their full attention before continuing. "The goal here is speed and stealth. We have to be quiet and we have to be quick. If we're not, there's a good chance I'll have a hole in my head by the end of the day."

That sobered up the room. Jack stood up again. "We won't let that happen."

Sadie smiled. "I know you won't. But either way, I'd like to go over some maneuvers before we get a good night's rest."

Cara stepped forward. "I know I'm not, like, a super-secret spy like you guys, but is there anything I can do to help?"

Sadie walked around the table and put a hand on the younger woman's shoulder. "I know this isn't what you want to hear, but the best thing you can do is stay safe. We'll put you up somewhere no one can find you, and then we'll come get you when all this is over."

Cara opened her mouth to argue, but Bear put his hand up. "She's right. We need you alive to blow this story wide open. We can't do it without you."

"You're just trying to flatter me, aren't you?"

Bear shrugged. "Maybe a little."

"I know you're right. I just feel...useless."

It was Jack's turn to step forward. "You helped get us this far. Don't undersell yourself. Being a super-secret spy isn't all it's cracked up to be."

"You get shot at a lot," Bear said.

Sadie groaned. "And put on desk duty."

Jack pointed a thumb at himself. "Or you're accused of being a terrorist."

Cara laughed. "I think I'll pass on at least two out of the three."

Sadie leaned forward, and in a loud whisper, she said, "Don't let these guys fool you. Desk duty is the worst one."

Jack shrugged. "It's true. Being accused of terrorism is actually pretty easy. You don't even have to do anything."

Bear clapped his hands together. It echoed through the space. "Okay, time to nail this down. I want to find both these brothers, take them out, and see what Vice President Eli Adams has to say for himself."

31

BEAR AND SADIE WERE STANDING IN THE SHADOWS OF THE LINCOLN memorial. Jack had just taken off toward Constitution Ave. They had half an hour before the meeting was meant to take place. Bear would've preferred to scope out the area ahead of time, but that ran the risk of alerting their adversaries to the idea that they knew something was going down.

So, he had relented. Cara was safe and sound in a nice hotel several blocks away that Sadie had set up for her. She was close enough that if there was an emergency, it would be easy to scoop her up and hightail it out of there. But she was also far enough to keep her away from the mess this was bound to turn into.

"I don't like it," Bear said.

"You've said that already," Sadie said.

"Well, I'm saying it again."

"You can say it as many times as you want, but it's not going to change anything."

"I know, but it makes me feel better."

Sadie rested a hand on his arm and smiled up at him. "I'm glad you're here."

There was a crackle in Bear's ear and Jack's voice came over the line. "What am I, chopped liver?"

Sadie scowled. "You're supposed to be concentrating."

"Hard to when you're getting all sentimental on us."

Sadie rolled her eyes and looked over at Bear, who grinned. The man sure knew how to ruin a moment, but Bear knew Sadie felt the same way he did. It wouldn't be the same without Jack Noble by their side.

Bear looked down at his watch. "How close are you, Jack?"

"Cleared the first building. Working on the second. There's a lot of goddamn stairs."

"You're getting lazy in your old age."

"Don't you worry about me, Big Man. I can still run circles around you."

Bear chuckled. "We're going to take our time walking to the island. Keep us posted."

"Copy that."

Bear looked over at Sadie, who pulled up the hood on her sweater. She was about Cara's size and had the same color hair. From a distance, and especially with Bear by her side, no one would suspect she was a body double. Up close, the two didn't look anything alike. The hood would at least delay that recognition a few precious seconds if they needed it.

But Bear hoped they wouldn't need it.

The two of them set off walking down the steps of the Memorial and beside the Reflecting Pool. The air was cold enough that Bear could see his breath on every exhale, but the direct sunlight worked to keep him warm, especially under the heavy winter jacket Sadie had picked up for him. She'd insisted on the pair of them wearing vests, and even though Bear hated how tight it fit him, he was thankful for the extra protection.

Even if it wasn't going to matter much.

The O'Reilly brothers weren't really the type to aim for the chest. They liked to put a bullet through the eye of their target every single time. That's why it was paramount that Jack made it to them before they set their sights on Sadie.

"How are you feeling?" Bear asked her.

Sadie kept her head on a swivel, but could only do so much with her hood obstructing her peripheral vision. "Good. Lots of energy. Glad to be out in the field again."

"Even if it's unsanctioned?"

"Maybe especially so." Sadie couldn't hide the glee in her voice.

On the record, Sadie had taken a well-deserved vacation. She'd kept her head down for so long that it was likely no one would grow suspicious, at least until it was too late. There was still a chance they had eyes on her and Bear, especially given the fact they were gearing up for a very public meeting with someone tied to the White House, but what other choice did they have?

Bear refrained from repeating the same line he'd said all morning.

"Building two is clear," Jack said over their headset. "Heading over to building three."

"We're coming to the end of the Pool. Starting toward the Gardens in about thirty seconds."

"Copy."

Jack had the hardest job of the three of them. There were only a handful of buildings where the O'Reilly brothers could set up their equipment. Sadie figured they'd have an all-access pass to everything on Constitution Ave since they were working for Hughes. Jack, on the other hand, would have to get creative.

Knowledge of the buildings was their biggest asset, and Jack had spent hours studying the maps Sadie had provided. Confidence also went a long way. If he couldn't pass through undetected, there was a good chance he'd be able to charm his way into any back staircases that might lead him to the rooftop of the building he was inspecting.

If he was quick and quiet about it, he'd be able to find at least one of the snipers before Bear and Sadie even entered the park. They had already pinged the buildings that would be ideal for a sniper setup. Jack was halfway through them, which meant it was only a matter of time.

For his part, Bear was keeping an eye out all around them. They entered the World War II Memorial at the end of the Pool and followed the outer wall until they hit a path that would lead them to their destination.

"Entering the Gardens," Bear whispered.

His earpiece crackled, but Jack didn't confirm.

Sadie glanced up at him with her eyebrow raised.

Bear shrugged but stayed attuned to whatever was happening on the other side of the line. If Jack didn't confirm, it could mean he'd spotted his target. That could either be great news for them, or bad news for Jack, depending on how it played out.

Sadie led them along the curved path toward the pond. They had already chosen to take the long way around so they could keep their eyes peeled for anyone who looked like they didn't belong. It would give them more time to scope the area. It would also give a sniper more time to line up their shot.

A grunt in his earpiece made Bear snap back to attention. He couldn't tell if it came from Jack or not. It was followed by a scuffle and surprised cry that cut off into a gurgle. Neither Bear nor Sadie visibly reacted to the sound, but he could tell they were both hyper-focused on what was going to come next.

It took about two heartbeats.

"Clear."

Jack's voiced was ragged, but solid. Bear could hear him breathing heavily and wondered if he was injured. It wouldn't slow him down much, but even a few seconds could be the difference between life and death.

Sadie was the first to speak. "What happened?"

"One of the brothers was on top of the third building. Had my eye on him for a while. I don't see a radio, so it looks like they weren't on comms. Probably wanted to avoid linking one to the other if one of them got caught."

Bear nodded his head ever so slightly. "If someone believed there was only one gunman, they wouldn't think to look for a second."

"But finding comms would change that," Sadie finished. "You okay?"

"I'm good. He landed one on me, but a knife through the throat will slow anyone down. I—"

Jack's voice faltered and Bear's heart skipped a beat. "What?"

"We got a problem." There was a rustle of paper. "He's got photos of his targets. Bear. Me. Sadie. Cara isn't even here."

"How does that make sense?" Sadie asked. "You'd think she'd be the prime target."

"I don't like it," Bear said, the implications crystalizing in his head.

Bear and Sadie were rounding the last curve of the lake. The path was just ahead of them now. There were several people crossing the bridge to the other side, and a few more milling about in the gardens. Any one of them could be their contact. Or the person sent there to kill them.

Sadie shook her head. "The willow trees are obstructing our view. I don't like the odds of walking onto that island without knowing exactly what's there."

Bear looked down at his watch. "We've got two minutes until noon."

"What happens if we're late?"

"We lose our shot of getting into contact with the VP?"

Sadie sighed and Bear knew she was thinking the same thing he was. They couldn't take that chance. Vice President Adams would be able to corroborate the evidence they found. He'd be able to put some power behind their accusations. Hughes could find a way to bury them, but not if they had Adams standing by their side.

They needed to make contact.

"We're got two minutes," Sadie said. "Let's hang back for a minute."

They stepped off the path and into the trees, circling slowly and keeping an eye on anyone coming from or going to the island. Most were tourists. A few were businessmen on lunch. No one looked especially out of the ordinary, but that didn't mean they weren't.

One minute, Sadie was walking alongside Bear, and the next, she was shoving him out of the way. A bang and a grunt followed her movements. Bear stumbled but stayed on his feet. Sadie went down, grasping her chest. Bear was by her side in a matter of seconds.

"Vest, vest," she said, ripping open her jacket and showing him where the bullets had landed. "Get him."

That was enough for Bear. With Sadie safe and recovering from the impact of being shot, Bear only had to worry about keeping himself safe. People were screaming and running. Jack was yelling in his ear. But Bear tuned it all out.

He had spotted the man with the gun. He had taken a few seconds too long to decide whether to keep shooting or to get out of there. When he saw Bear charging toward him, he raised his weapon, but Bear was already diving behind a tree.

The man's first mistake was shooting Sadie. The second was believing he could outrun Bear. At a dead sprint and over a short track, Bear was fast. By the time he hit top speed, he was already at the man's ankles. It was definitely the other O'Reilly brother.

Bear tackled him to the ground. The other man was smaller and quicker than Bear had expected. As soon as he hit the dirt, he was already pushing himself back up again. He swung the gun toward Bear's head and looked down at him with a grin.

One minute he was smiling, and the next, there were three bullets in his face.

Bear rolled to the side and brought his own weapon out, pointing it at the source of the gunfire. He only lowered it once he recognized Sadie, who stood with both feet planted and her gun still aimed at the man on the ground.

Bear waited for her to start moving toward him. "He's dead."

Jack's voice was loud in Bear's ear. "Will someone tell me what the fuck is going on?"

"The other shooter is down." Sadie's voice was still ragged, like it hurt to breathe too deeply. "The meeting has been compromised. I don't think anyone is coming out of the woodwork to talk with us now. We need to move before the cops get here."

Bear could already hear sirens in the distance.

"I think we've got a bigger problem than the cops," Jack said.

Bear could hear it in his voice. He was thinking the same thing Bear was.

Sadie was brave enough to ask the question. "What?"

"This whole meeting was a setup. It was to get us away from Cara. She's the real target. She's the one they're really after."

Bear didn't respond. He couldn't. He just took off running in the direction of the hotel. He didn't want to even imagine the worst-case scenario, but years of living this life meant it was easy to drum up those images. Cara could be dead. Or worse.

Losing her meant losing another person who could speak to Hughes' ulterior motives.

It also meant more blood on Bear's hands.

And that, more than anything, he didn't think he could live with.

32

Bear didn't bother being discreet. Time wasn't on their side, and he needed every second he could get. Once they got to the hotel, they wouldn't be able to stay. Didn't matter what he found there. He needed to get in and out as fast as possible.

With Cara in tow.

He heard Sadie and Jack shouting through the earpiece he was still wearing. Bear ignored them. He had a one-track mind, and right now, it was focused on making sure Cara Bishop was safe and sound where they had last left her.

He barreled through the revolving doors of the hotel, ignoring the startled bellhop standing by to help guests with their luggage. Bear didn't bother with the elevators. He took the stairs three at a time up to the eighth floor. His lungs burned. His head felt light. He bent over and caught his breath.

Bear pulled out his pistol, pointed it at the floor. He ran the risk of startling the other hotel guests, but that was a chance he was willing to take. The other option was not having enough time to retrieve his weapon if he needed it. That outcome led to certain death.

He pulled open the door to the eighth floor and stuck his head through the opening. He looked left, and then right, and then left again. No one was in the hallway. The entire level was quiet.

It didn't put him at ease.

He heard footsteps in the stairwell several floors down. They echoed up to where he had paused in the doorway. They could've been Jack's or Sadie's, but he didn't want to run the risk of it being someone else. He slipped through the doorway and let it click shut behind him.

They had put Cara in a room of her own halfway down the hall. They sprang for a nicer hotel to make her feel safer and more comfortable. Security was also tighter in a building like this. They had cameras and security guards, unlike the places she and Bear had been staying the last couple nights. They hadn't been too worried about her. Why would anyone go looking for a girl they knew would be at the contact point at noon?

Because they had somehow known about the switch, which meant everything they thought they knew about the meeting had just gone out the window.

The door to Cara's room was closed. A *do not disturb* sign was hanging off the handle. He had told her to keep the curtains drawn and the lights off. Don't make a lot of noise. Sleep as much as possible. Try not to worry about what was going on outside these four walls.

Bear pulled a keycard out of his back pocket and listened as the lock clicked open. He waited a beat, but when he didn't hear any noise on the other side, he swung the door open and aimed his pistol forward.

Whatever he had been expecting, it was so much worse.

The entire room was trashed, from top to bottom. The blankets and sheets had been pulled off the bed and strewn onto the floor. The television was tipped over, along with the chair. Even the bathroom had been turned over.

What had they been looking for? A flash drive full of information? One of Cara's notebooks? Any indication that she had hidden some information that could be used against Hughes if it got into the wrong hands? All three options were likely scenarios.

What made everything worse was the amount of blood on the floor. Cara wasn't a fighter, which meant she either got extremely lucky, or everything on the ground was from her. Had this occurred as they tried to get her out of the room, or had they tortured her for information? He didn't dwell on it.

Bear made his way through the room, looking for any evidence. The gun they had left for her in the drawer was still there, untouched. He had warned her not to order any room service and not to open the door for anyone but him. That meant someone had probably opened the door with a keycard.

Someone in the hotel had given away her position.

Bear heard footsteps down the hallway and turned in time to see Sadie cross the threshold of the room. Her eyes went wide as she took in the scene. Bear didn't bother explaining his conclusions to her. He saw her make the same assumptions within seconds of going through the room herself.

"Jack thinks the guy at the front desk gave her away."

Bear didn't respond. He just followed Sadie out of the room and back down the stairs, tucking his gun away as he went. He recalled the kid who had been behind the desk as they had checked in. Bear and Jack had been sitting in the lounge area while Sadie had checked in with Cara. The two of them had gone upstairs, and ten minutes later, Bear and Jack had followed. Nothing had seemed out of the ordinary at the time.

Now he was kicking himself for not being more vigilant.

"Don't do that," Sadie said.

"Do what?"

"Blame yourself for this. I can see it in your eyes. You're pissed."

"Damn right I am."

"It's not your fault, Bear. Everything is against us here. We knew there was little chance this wasn't going to go sideways."

Bear didn't respond. That was true, and Bear had resigned himself to the idea that he, Jack, or Sadie might be taken down in the process. That was the job. That was the life. But Cara deserved better than this. She deserved more than he had provided her.

Sadie shook her head, probably knowing nothing she could say would change how Bear felt. He was grateful she didn't push the matter. He'd feel better once they found Cara—preferably alive—and had Hughes in handcuffs.

Sadie pushed through the door at the bottom of the stairs and walked out into the lobby. She made a beeline to the entrance of a small room behind the check-in counter and Bear followed close behind her. There was a small line of people waiting to be checked in, and Bear assumed it was because Jack was keeping the concierge employee otherwise occupied.

And as soon as Bear walked into the back, he saw that he was right.

The kid was maybe twenty-five years old. Jack had him sitting in a swivel chair in the middle of the room. He wasn't tied down, but by the way he was gripping the arms of the chair, Bear assumed Jack had threatened to do something inventive if he tried to bolt.

Sometimes that held better than any length of rope.

"Did you have to break his nose?" Sadie said. "We're trying to keep a low profile."

"We're also short on time," Jack said. He turned back to the kid. "Okay, Marcus. Tell my friends what you told me."

Marcus didn't even hesitate. "I got a phone call yesterday from one of our contacts who sets up rooms on behalf of certain politicians. Sometimes they tell us the names and sometimes they don't, depending on who it is. If it's someone big, they'll use a fake name. But depending on who calls to set it up, you can usually narrow it down to a few obvious choices."

"Get to the point," Bear said.

Marcus grimaced as he licked his lips. "Yesterday, one of the contacts called. Didn't say who was staying here. We've talked a few times. She knows I'm a good employee, that I keep my mouth shut. I've seen a lot of things they wouldn't want to get out into the papers, you know? But they slip me a couple hundred dollars and I keep it to myself."

Jack turned to Bear. "Loyalty isn't really Marcus' thing. He does like money, though."

"I have a lot of student loans. I—"

"Save it." Bear took a step forward. "I don't give a shit. Keep talking."

"The lady on the phone said her boss was going to surprise his niece, but that he couldn't remember which hotel she was staying in. They were calling all the local hotels trying to figure out. She sent over a picture of the girl. Said I'd get a grand out of it if I told them when she showed up and which room she was staying in."

Bear crossed his arms over his chest. "And you didn't think that was strange?"

"I don't know, man. Not really. You'd be surprised the things they get up to in here."

"I really wouldn't."

"I thought it was kind of nice, you know?" Marcus shifted in his seat, but never stopped gripping the arms of the chair. "I wanted to help."

"I bet the thousand dollars didn't hurt either."

"Look, I'm sorry—"

"Save it," Bear said.

Sadie stepped forward. "The woman on the phone, who did she normally represent?"

"Lots of people," Marcus said. "But she usually sets up appointments for the bigwigs."

"Like who?"

Marcus shook his head. "Lots of people. I've seen the attorney general a couple times. The secretary of defense. Even the Vice President showed up once. But I only knew that because my cousin saw him in the hallway. They always come in a back entrance."

Bear had already tuned him out. He looked at Sadie, and then at Jack.

"It's him. He has her." Bear couldn't help the way he spit out the man's title like it was poison. "The Vice President has been in on it from the beginning."

33

"SO, WHAT'S THE PLAN?"

Jack was sitting in the driver's seat of a panel van Sadie had rented for them. Someone had smoked in it recently, and it smelled like a mix of ash and corn chips. It was a little more conspicuous than Bear would've liked, but the extra room for all their gear was a nice addition. They were going to need it.

Sadie was sitting in the passenger's seat. She had taken her hood off and removed her vest. There were already a couple of purple bruises blossoming across her chest. They were going to hurt like hell for a few days, but it was better than the alternative.

Bear was in the back of the van, sitting in a seat against one of the walls. He didn't want to be cooped up back there, but between the scene in the park and the scene at the hotel, they all figured it'd be better to keep their faces hidden for a while.

But just thinking about the hotel made him want to start punching things.

"What's the plan?" Jack asked again.

"I don't know," Bear said.

"We need to find Hughes," Sadie said.

"But Adams has the girl," Bear said. "We should be going after him?"

"The Vice President of the United States?" Sadie's voice was even, but Bear could detect the incredulity. "He's untouchable."

"No one is untouchable."

"Well, he's as close as it gets."

"I gotta agree with Sadie," Jack said. When he noticed Bear's glare, he held up his hands. "But the VP isn't our only problem."

"Then we go after Hughes," Bear said. "And he leads us to Adams."

"Hughes is hardly a better target." Sadie and Jack must've exchanged a look because she continued with a much more positive note in her voice. "But there is a chance we can get to him."

Bear took a deep breath. He had to reign it in. He didn't ignore the rage building inside him. It was useful. But he did have to compartmentalize it. Now was the time for a clear head and a plan of action. The anger would come in later when it was time to get the job done.

"How?" Bear asked. "How can we get to the Director of National Intelligence?"

"You said he goes home to his wife every night, right? We stake out his house."

Jack shook his head. "Look, I'm all for this plan, but this guy isn't going to be easy to get alone in a room. We gotta be careful. He's gonna have all kinds of security."

"So, we take it out." Bear was already thinking about what weapons he was going to bring along.

"That's all fair and good," Sadie said. "But we need to be smart about this. His wife is probably going to be home. He could have men stationed around his house that have no idea what's going on here. They'll be innocent."

It sounded like she added that part for Bear's sake.

He got the message.

"Okay," Sadie said. "So, how do we be smart about this?"

Both Sadie and Bear turned to Jack.

"Brandon can get his address. He can probably also find work records to figure out what sort of security system he has. Might be able to crack it remotely, or he can tell us how to do it on-site."

"He's not going to like that," Bear said. "We've already tapped Brandon for what he's worth."

"Let me handle him," Jack said. "We'll have to scope the area to figure out who's stationed there, either out in the open or under-cover. Hughes has been doing some shady shit for quite a while now, which means his men are probably dirty, too. But since we don't know that for sure, we'll have to incapacitate and secure them. After that, we just have to get to Hughes and his wife."

"I'd prefer to get Hughes alone," Sadie said. "He might be more unpredictable if he's worried about her safety. We want the most ideal scenario for interrogation."

"Which won't be easy," Bear said. "He's a military man. He's the Director of National Security."

"But there's three of us and one of him," Jack said. "I like our odds."

Bear agreed. "Nothing to do now but get it done."

Jack and Sadie looked at each other and then back to Bear. They nodded in unison.

It was time.

NIGHT HAD FALLEN AND BEAR, Jack, and Sadie were huddled in the back of the panel van parked a few blocks down from Hughes' brownstone. Brandon had come through for them, obtaining the man's home address, the layout to his house, and the work orders for his security system. He had sent everything to Sadie's phone, which was a bit more sophisticated than what Jack and Bear usually carried.

"The house is pretty straightforward," Sadie said, holding her phone close to her face. "It's got two floors and a basement. Everything flows from one room to the other. We should be able to clear it pretty quickly with just the three of us."

Jack didn't take his eyes off the 9mm he was inspecting. "Any indication of a panic room?"

"None, but I wouldn't discount it."

"He probably wouldn't want that to be on any blueprints that might get into the wrong hands," Bear said.

Sadie hummed her agreement. "Next up is the security system. Brandon said he's got 24-hour detail at the front gate. Just one guard. The digital security system is a completely different story. It's...complicated."

"With any luck, we won't have to deal with that," Jack said.

Bear checked his watch. "Brandon should be calling any second now."

As if on cue, Jack's phone lit up. He put it on speaker and placed it between the three of them. "We're all here, Brandon. What you got for us?"

Brandon hesitated. "Honestly, I'm not sure."

Bear and Sadie exchanged looks.

"Good news or bad news?" Jack asked.

"A bit of both."

"Fill us in," Bear said. He was trying to keep his voice even, but as the hours dragged on, his patience got thinner and thinner.

Brandon cleared his throat. "Hughes' system is run by Star Security. They're a top tier security system. Hacking into them wasn't difficult, but going about it undetected was the hard part."

Jack leaned forward. "I'm guessing you were successful?"

"I was." Something squeaked in the background while Brandon shifted in his seat. "Long story short, think of Star Security as an entire house full of doors. On the first floor, all the doors require a normal everyday metal key to open their locks. The second floor required a four-digit code. The third floor required a six-digit code and so on."

"Which level is Hughes' account on?" Sadie asked.

"We're talking the fifteenth level. He requires a security code and a retina scanner. The whole nine."

"Is there any good news here?" Bear asked.

"The good news is I cracked the code to get onto his floor. The *strange* news is that his door was already open."

Bear looked up at Jack, who's expression matched his own.

"How is that even possible?" Sadie asked.

"I don't know. There should be alarm bells screaming at me right now," Brandon said. "But everything is quiet."

Bear shifted closer to the phone. "What do you think happened? Best guess."

Brandon sighed. The static crackled on the phone, distorting his voice for a word or two. "Best guess? Someone beat us to the punch. They hacked their way into their system and shut down his security. But they didn't bother closing the door behind them because they stopped any notifications from going on."

Sadie asked, "What do you mean by notifications?"

"Okay, imagine every door also comes with a security dog. When the door is opened, the dog starts barking. If he recognizes the intruder, like someone who works at Star Security, he stops barking and no alarms go off."

"So, you think the hacker works at the company?" Bear asked.

"That was my first guess," Brandon said. "But I'm looking through the log right now, and there's no record of anyone opening this door. It's like they wiped the whole thing. The only way Star Security would know something was wrong would be if someone manually checked this account."

"Who could do something like this?" Jack asked.

"Me." Brandon laughed. "With enough time, I could've done this. Maybe a couple other guys I know, but the list is short."

"Any of them on a first name basis with the Vice President?" Bear asked.

"These guys don't really like doing what the government tells them to, if you know what I mean."

Jack sat up straighter. "It doesn't matter who did it. We need to know when. You said there are records of everything that happened on the account?"

"Yep, one second." Brandon whistled a couple notes that came through the phone high-pitched and shrill. "Looks like Hughes came home at 7:03 p.m. Nothing else is recorded until 10:17 p.m., when he set the night protocols. It's been, what, an hour since then? There's no indication when the system went dark."

"If the guard or anyone else had been alerted to the breech," Sadie said, "the cops would be all over this area."

Bear looked out the back window, as if he could see all the way into Hughes' bedroom window. "This is our chance. We're not going to get another one."

"We have no idea if or when the security system will come back online," Sadie argued. "We'll be going in blind against a timer we can't see."

"Brandon, can you keep an eye on police channels? Let us know if anyone gets dispatched to Hughes' address?" Bear asked.

"Sure can."

Bear looked first at Sadie and then at Jack. "All we'll need is a two-minute head start. No one will know we're there."

"Good enough for me," Jack said.

Sadie threw up her hands. "We have no idea what we're walking into there."

"We know we only have to deal with one guard, a downed security system, and a sixty-year-old man and his wife."

"That sixty-year-old man is the Director of National Intelligence. And if he's not dead already, then whoever shut down his security system could still be in there with him."

Bear grinned. "Then let's go thank them for a job well done."

34

BEAR WAITED AROUND THE CORNER AND OUT OF SIGHT WHILE JACK and Sadie made their way down the sidewalk and toward the brownstone. Bear had wanted to be the first one through the door but relented when Jack pointed out how conspicuous he was.

"Conspicuous, my ass," Bear said, leaning up against the cold brick of an apartment building.

But Jack wasn't wrong.

Instead, Jack and Sadie were arm in arm as they stumbled down the block, doing their best impersonation of a couple of D.C. natives who may have let off a little too much steam after work. They were laughing and shouting, not at all trying to blend in.

Sometimes the best disguises were the most obvious.

Bear couldn't make out the words, but he could tell when they had finally reached the outside of the brownstone. It had a low gate they could've easily hopped, but not before the guard had pulled his weapon on them.

The plan was simple. Sadie and Jack would say hello to the guard, who would tell them to move on. When they refused, the guard would choose to step forward instead of drawing his weapons on a couple of civilians. Once he was in range, then Jack would—

Two short whistles indicated Jack had been successful in knocking out the guard.

Bear pushed off the building, tucked his hands deep into the pocket of his winter coat, and headed toward the brownstone. He kept his eyes peeled for any movement that indicated they were being watched.

When he reached Jack and Sadie, the two of them had already pulled the guard inside.

"Door was unlocked," Sadie said. "You two clear the first and second floor. I'll keep an eye on the front door."

"What about the basement?" Bear asked.

"I'll hold it," she said. "Once we know the living areas are clear, we'll make that our next priority."

"Copy that," Jack said. "I'll take the first floor."

"I'll take the second," Bear said.

And just like that, the three of them parted ways. Bear climbed the stairs to the second floor while keeping his back to the wall. He watched the landing above him, but there was no movement. The whole house was dead silent.

It was bigger than Waller's home, but he had cleared that one on his own. He was glad to have Jack and Sadie with him this time. It wasn't just about safety. They kept him grounded. They kept him smart. Three heads were always better than one.

When Bear hit the landing, he pulled up a mental image of the house's blueprints. There were a handful of rooms up here, as well as a couple of bathrooms. He methodically cleared them all, checking the closets and under the bed. He saved the master bedroom for last.

Satisfied that every other room was empty, Bear moved to the last door in the hallway. He half-expected it to be locked, but when he twisted the handle and pushed it open, it swung silently on the hinges.

And immediately he knew something was wrong.

Mrs. Hughes was lying in bed with the covers pulled up to her chest. She easily could've been sleeping, if her eyes hadn't been open and her mouth hadn't been slack. Bear didn't see any blood, but that didn't mean there wasn't any.

Before he checked the body, Bear cleared the bathroom, the closet, and under the bed. Everything seemed to be in place. It was all spotless. Organized. Ordinary.

Bear peeled back the covers to check the rest of Mrs. Hughes' body. There was no blood. No sign of a struggle he could discern. If he had to guess, the assailant had snuck into the room and put a pillow over her face while she slept. Hughes hadn't been in the room, or the crime scene would've been messier.

Bear flipped the covers back over the body and headed downstairs, meeting Jack at the base of the steps.

"All clear," Jack said as Sadie joined them.

"Got a body upstairs," Bear said. "The wife. Probably suffocated in her sleep. No blood. No evidence."

"And Hughes?" Sadie asked.

"Nowhere to be found."

The three of them turned simultaneously to the basement.

Jack checked his phone. "Brandon says it's still clear, but I'm starting to feel the hairs on the back of my neck stand up. Let's make this quick."

Bear didn't need to be told twice. He walked over to the basement door and waited for Jack and Sadie to line up behind him. He held up three fingers and counted down to one before he pulled it open and began to descend the stairs, quietly but quickly. He felt the others on his heels.

Unlike the rest of the house, the basement seemed alive. The lights were on, and Bear heard the subtle buzz of a computer whirring somewhere across the room. He immediately spotted a figure in a chair in front of a desk, and while he kept his gun trained on him, the other two cleared the rest of the area.

When they returned with the all-clear, Bear moved closer to the man in the chair. But it didn't matter. It had been apparent since the descent down the stairs that Hughes was dead. A single bullet wound had entered the left side of his head and exited the right, staining the wall with brain and blood.

Sadie followed the trajectory of the bullet. "Looks like the shooter stood right behind him and shot him."

"Point blank." Bear looked at the rest of the man's body. He was in his pajamas, but nothing looked out of place. "I'm guessing the killer came in and went directly to his room, killing his wife. When he didn't find Hughes there, he headed down here. Found him on the computer."

"He must've been surprised," Jack said. "He wasn't expecting anyone since he had already set the alarms for the night."

"But whoever it was must've gotten the jump on him," Bear continued. "He didn't have a weapon. There's no sign of a struggle. He must've gotten what he wanted and killed him with a silencer, otherwise the guard outside would've heard the shot."

Sadie walked back over to them. "So, what did the killer want?"

Bear took in the scene before him. He knew they had limited time, but this was their only chance to get some answers. They had to take advantage of it. Bear pointed to the cell phone lying on the desk. "Sadie, you grab his cell. See if there's anything useful in there. I'll get the computer. Jack, get on the phone with Brandon. See if he's figured out who could've done this."

Sadie and Jack followed Bear's lead. Everyone was aware of the pressure of time. They did not want to be here when the authorities showed up. Once they were dispatched, it would only take a few minutes for this entire sector of the neighborhood to be locked down. They had to be long-gone before then.

Bear didn't move Hughes' body as he reached over to work on the computer. Gloves would've been ideal, but they hadn't had time to pick up extra supplies. They'd have to wipe down the phone and the computer before they left.

Hughes had two monitors set up on a desk that was void of any decoration. He didn't even have a picture of his wife and kids down here. This was a workstation that was not meant to be mixed up with any personal memorabilia.

Bear could tell just by looking at the tower sitting on the ground that the computer was powerful. Hughes would have the best of the best, and it'd normally be locked down tighter than Fort Knox. Luckily, Hughes had been working when he was killed, which means Bear had access to just about everything in Hughes' system.

The left monitor only had one window open. It was an inbox filled with messages from a single person. Like any good spy or criminal, Hughes and whoever he had been corresponding with didn't use their real names. Hughes' moniker was Whitefish. His pen pal was named Cobra.

Bear skimmed the emails, but it was like walking into the middle of a conversation. You got a general sense of what was going on, but without knowing context, most of it went right over his head. It seemed Hughes and Cobra had been having a bit of a disagreement. While Hughes wanted to slow down their plan, Cobra wanted to stick to their original timetable, even though London hadn't gone according to plan and Jack was still in the wind.

Sadie walked over to Bear and set the phone back on the desk after wiping it clean with her shirt. "I've got nothing."

Bear looked up from the computer. "Really?"

"It's probably the phone he takes to work every day, so it was pretty clean. Probably didn't want to risk someone getting their hands on it."

"Makes sense." Bear turned back to the monitor with the emails. "He probably did most of his communication here, where he had the most control over who got into his house, who got into his basement, and who had access to his computer."

"Find anything interesting?"

"Oh yeah." Bear gestured at the screen. "But I'm not sure what any of it means. Hughes' codename with his partner was White-fish. Whoever he was working with was named—"

"Cobra." Sadie's face had gone pale.

"You recognize the names?"

"Yes." Sadie leaned toward the computer. "I spent the past several months tracking a plot to attack several tankers in the Persian Gulf. We didn't have much, but we managed to piece together two codenames: Whitefish and Cobra."

35

Jack joined them around the computer. He was still on the phone with Brandon. "We've got to go. Brandon says they just dispatched a fleet of patrol cars to this address. Anonymous tip."

Bear grabbed the phone from Jack. "If you can get remote access to a computer system, can you download a series of emails without leaving a trace?"

"I can download a lot more than that." There was a hint of excitement in Brandon's voice.

"Tell me how."

Brandon walked Bear through the steps. It only took a couple clicks and a few keystrokes, and Brandon was in the system. "In a couple hours, we'll have everything we ever wanted to know about Director Mason Hughes."

Bear couldn't help the grin that spread across his face. "Good shit."

"Bear." Sadie's voice was sober. She was pointing to the other monitor—the one Bear hadn't had a chance to look at yet. There was a map with a blinking red dot in the center. "Hughes was tracking someone."

Bear leaned closer. "Do we know who it is?"

Sadie shook her head. "Could be Cara."

Bear didn't want to get his hopes up. "Could be Cobra."

"Either way," Jack said, "if Hughes was interested in tracking whoever this is, we should be, too."

Bear held the phone closer to his mouth. "Brandon?"

"On it."

Bear knew Brandon enjoyed this—it was as close to the action as he ever got—but he also knew they were getting close to tapping out on favors from their own personal computer genius. They'd have to repay it in kind sooner rather than later.

But that was a problem for a different day.

"You guys need to get moving," Brandon said. "You've got two minutes. If you go out the back and circle around, you should be fine."

"We'll have to switch cars soon," Jack said.

"Let's jump that hurdle when we get there." Sadie was already heading up the stairs. "First, we need to get out of this house."

Bear didn't argue, though part of him wanted to stay and study the map more. If the tracking device was Cara, this might be their only chance to track her down. But he had to trust in Brandon. His computer skills were unmatched, and he'd be able to get the location within a matter of minutes.

Right now they had other priorities.

Bear hung up with Brandon and wiped down the keyboard and mouse with his shirt. He followed Sadie up the stairs and out the back door. He looked back only once, to make sure the guard was still tied to the bannister where they had left him. He was conscious now, but Jack had taken a towel from the kitchen and covered the man's eyes. He might be able to identify Jack or Sadie, but with the security system down and the fact that it had been dark out, Bear liked their chances.

Bear matched Sadie's strides as they crept through Hughes' backyard and down the block. "Tell me more about Whitefish and Cobra."

"About two days after I came to your apartment, I got an anonymous email from someone who said London was part of something bigger. We get tips all the time, but this one came to me directly. They knew about London. They knew about Korea. Something told me it was either a setup or the truth."

"What made you decide which was which?"

Sadie tucked a piece of hair behind her ear and chuckled. "I'm not sure. I decided to go out on a limb, I guess. I was planning on keeping my head down, so I sat on it for a while. They emailed again. This time it was only two words."

"Whitefish and Cobra," Bear said.

Jack was ahead of them, his head on a swivel, but Bear could tell he was listening in.

"So, I did some digging. Kept it off the radar. Didn't tell anyone about it. Didn't come up with anything."

"They emailed again?"

"Yeah. This time, they pointed to the Persian Gulf. I didn't find anything labeled Whitefish and Cobra, but I did find some intelligence regarding a possible attack. I figured I didn't have to bring up the codenames. I just needed to relay the information. There was enough there to require a deeper look."

"Why do I feel like there's a *but* coming along?"

"*But*," Sadie said, a humorless smile on her face, "my boss ignored it. Said someone would look into it and then shoved it at the bottom of the pile."

"He was burying it."

"*She* was burying it, yes. So, I stuck my neck out. Gave it to her boss. He decided it was worth looking into. We've been gathering evidence ever since."

Jack dropped back a step or two. "What did you find?"

"Lots of buzz about the tankers in the Persian Gulf. There's a plan to light them all up."

"Seems in line with Hughes' master plan," Bear said. "That'll do a lot of damage to the oil industry and it'll definitely have an effect on Saudi Arabia and other countries in the area."

"First London," Jack said. "Then Germany. Now the Gulf. This was Hughes' next hit. After this, he'd either need to go bigger or start going public, blaming it on some sort of terrorist organization. He knew we were onto him, so he needed to start getting the people on his side. If he could start a war, it'd be much easier to use the chaos as a cover for anything else he had planned."

"But Hughes wanted to slow the whole thing down. He wanted to lay low. The emails made it sound like he wanted to go quiet for a while."

"Cold feet?" Sadie asked.

"No, he still wanted to go through with the plan. He just wanted to delay it. Cobra didn't."

Sirens drew closer. They each picked up the pace. The van was within sight now. They just had to get in and drive away without being noticed by the cops. Hopefully the urgency of the anonymous tip would mean they wouldn't pay attention to a single van sitting alongside the road several blocks away.

"And we're assuming Cobra is the Vice President?" Sadie asked.

"He's clearly a part of this plan," Bear said. "But how much, I'm not sure yet."

"If he is," Jack said, "then he's clearly tying up loose ends.

Waller, Mateo, and Hughes are all dead. They were all close enough to the plan that they'd be able to pin it on him. If he and Hughes were worried about getting caught, Adams might be cutting his losses and going for a Hail Mary."

"And Cara Bishop is just another loose end," Bear said.

The other two didn't say anything. They were all thinking the same thing. The chance that she was still alive was pretty slim. It would take a miracle to find her in time.

Or maybe just a computer genius.

Bear reached the van first and did a preliminary look along the underside of the vehicle. He didn't spot any devices, either tracking or explosive. When he opened the side door, Sadie jumped in and Jack circled around to the driver's seat.

Then the phone rang. Jack put it on speaker. Brandon's voice filled the small area. There was a hint of urgency in his voice. "Good news and bad news."

"Hit us with it," Jack said.

"The good news is that I got some of what was on Hughes' computer."

"Some?" Bear asked.

"That's the bad news. Whoever killed him must've uploaded a virus. It was systematically deleting all the information on his hard drive by the time I got in there. If you guys had been even just a few minutes later, we might not have gotten anything."

"So, what did you get?" Sadie asked.

"I managed to download some communication logs, the emails, and a few other things. I'll have to go through it all before I really know what we got."

"And the map with the tracker?" Bear asked.

"That was the last thing that downloaded before it all went blank. I found the tracker's history log and plugged in a handful of the coordinates it had visited most often. Looks like Hughes was tracking this person for quite some time without him knowing."

"Who is it?"

"Between the White House and his home address, it could only be one person." Brandon took a deep breath and exhaled. "The Vice President."

36

Jack had wasted no time pulling away from the curb and heading in the opposite direction of Hughes' brownstone. As soon as Brandon gave them the coordinates to the beacon's current location, Jack was navigating side roads toward their destination.

Brandon told them satellite images indicated it was an abandoned building just outside of the city. The tracker had been there for about an hour already, which meant Adams hadn't been the one to pull the trigger on Hughes. Instead, he had probably hired the assassin, just like he'd hired the person to take down Hughes' security system. Maybe they were one and the same.

Halfway to their destination, they had abandoned the van and transferred everything to a navy blue 2002 Blazer that Sadie had hotwired faster than Bear and Jack could gather their weapons. When they both raised an eyebrow at her, she just shrugged and got behind the wheel.

Now, they were sitting outside a derelict structure that housed the Vice President of the United States. Bear had a feeling Cara would be inside, but whether she was still alive was a completely different story. Did Adams have a bunch of men with him, too, or was he flying solo? How many people could he truly trust at this stage in his operation?

After about ten minutes of surveillance, Bear was getting antsy. They didn't see anyone go in or out. Brandon told them Adams was still inside, but he couldn't tell them where in the building he was. He might've been on the ground floor, the fourth floor, or anywhere in between.

They'd be going in blind.

But Bear was good with that. When he told Jack and Sadie as much, they didn't argue. It was time to stop running and bring the fight to the man who had kept them chasing their tails since they first landed in Costa Rica. It seemed like a lifetime ago.

Bear tucked his 9mm in his waistband and took a shotgun Sadie handed him. The plan was simple: Go in hot, do as much damage as possible without getting shot themselves, and corner Adams. After that, they'd have to wing it.

None of them had ever held the Vice President of the United States at gunpoint before. They weren't sure what to expect. Would he cower, or would he fight back? Adams wasn't a military man like Hughes, but that didn't mean he wasn't dangerous. Everything that led to this moment had proven he was capable of some truly terrible things.

Bear, Sadie, and Jack loaded up and hopped out of the vehicle. The three of them exchanged a look but didn't say anything. They didn't need to. They had all been in this from the beginning. Jack and Bear had a long history, but now that was intertwined with Sadie, too. Nothing any of them could say would be enough.

So, they just let the moment hang in the air.

"I'll go around back," Sadie said after their moment of silence. "You two hit the front."

"Copy that," Jack said. "Let's end this."

That was enough of a signal for Bear. While Sadie circled the building and took the back entrance, he and Jack stayed low and approached the abandoned building in front of them.

It was made of brick and every one of the windows was boarded up. It was four stories high. Bear wasn't sure if it had a basement, but he figured they'd tackle that problem when they got to it. Right now, it was just about getting inside the door and seeing what they were up against.

The front only had one entrance, offset to the right. Without any viable windows, they'd be charging in blind, but Jack and Bear were used to bad odds. They'd made it out okay so far.

Then again, both of them were wanted fugitives. It seemed *okay* was a relative term.

They stuck to the shadows until they were flush with the façade. Though the boarded-up windows meant they couldn't see inside the building, it also meant Adams and whoever else was in there wouldn't be able to see their approach either. The element of surprise was on their side.

Jack crept closer to the door and paused. Bear was on his heels and stopped when he did. If there was any noise inside, they couldn't hear it. Maybe no one was talking. Or maybe no one was on the first floor. Maybe the bricks just muffled everyone's voices.

Either way, the silence only served to enhance the eeriness of the building's broken body.

Jack held up his hand and counted down from five. On the final number, he grabbed the handle to the front door and pulled it open. It creaked on its hinges, but Bear had expected as much. They weren't going for stealth this time. They were going for brute force.

He aimed his shotgun at chest-level and pushed through the door.

Three men stood in a circle in the center of a room that was devoid of any furniture whatsoever. The boards on the floor were soft with age and rot, and the entire building smelled like mold. The only light came from a couple of bright lanterns tucked into the corners. It was just enough to see by.

Bear only hesitated for a fraction of a second. He wasn't going to shoot an unarmed man, but as soon as he saw them raise their weapons, he pulled the trigger on his own. The crack of the shotgun echoed throughout the building, and he immediately heard footsteps above him.

Bear took down the man on the right, while Jack put a bullet in the head of the man on the left. They met in the middle and each of them got a piece of the remaining guy. He stumbled backward and crumpled to the ground with nothing more than a grunt.

Sadie made her entrance and the three of them stood in what used to be an apartment building. All the walls had been gutted and now it was just one large room. There was a staircase on each side leading to the next level. They would have to split up.

"Heard movement as soon as we made our entrance," Jack said.

"Me too. Can't tell how many are up there," Bear said.

"There are three SUVs out back, so I'd expect a decent team." She looked around the room. Doesn't seem to be any stairs leading down. They're all above us."

"Jack and I will take the left and draw their fire. You go up the right and hit them from behind. We clear the room quickly and keep moving. If Cara is here, who knows what they'll do once they know we're after her."

Jack and Sadie nodded, taking up their positions at the bottom of the stairs on each side of the room. When Bear joined Jack, he gave the signal and the three of them moved steadily up the staircase. Bear switched to his pistol halfway up. With Sadie on the other side and who knows what else going on up there, precision would be key.

Jack's head cleared the landing first and the shooting began immediately. Jack fired two shots in quick succession, and Bear heard bodies drop to the floor. From the other side of the building, he heard Sadie fire another three, followed by thuds.

By the time Bear cleared the landing and got a good look at the room, most of the team was already down.

Someone screamed above them.

Bear didn't waste any time. While Jack and Sadie finished off the remaining men on the second floor, he launched himself up the stairs. He didn't know Cara well, but who else could it have been? The scream had belonged to a woman and she sounded terrified. But at least he knew she was alive.

For now.

When he cleared the third-floor landing, Bear was met with exactly what he had feared.

Cara was tied to a chair, her head hanging so her chin rested against her chest. There was blood everywhere, and it seemed like one of her arms sat at a strange angle. Her face was a palette of purple. The only thing that told Bear she was still alive was the subtle rise and fall of her chest.

A man stood to her left, his knuckles bloody. His grin twisted his face into a mask of horrific glee. Across the room, Adams stood with his back to the other staircase. He looked more angry than scared. It was a telling sign of the man's character. He wasn't afraid of Bear; he was angry that Bear had gotten in his way.

Two men stood between them. Before they could even turn their guns on Bear, Bear put a bullet in their chests. They crumpled to the floor while Adams took a surprised step backwards. It caught him off guard, but it also gave the last remaining goon time to draw his weapon.

But he didn't draw it on Bear. Instead, he drew it on Cara.

Bear had Adams in his sights. One minuscule squeeze of the trigger would end everything. The conspiracy. The attack in the Gulf. And all of Bear's troubles. Or, at least, most of them.

But it would also end Cara's life. There was no way he could take out Adams before the other man pulled his own trigger.

Adams must've come to the same conclusion because he recovered quickly. With a smile on his face, he stood a little bit taller. He even straightened his tie.

"Her or me?" he said. "Who's it going to be?"

Bear didn't hesitate. He had made his decision when they pulled up to the abandoned building. They knew Adams was here, but they had been hoping Cara was, too. This was a rescue mission. If they took Adams down in the process, all the better.

So, instead of pulling the trigger right away, Bear swung his 9mm toward the man standing next to Cara and squeezed off two bullets. One tore through the man's left cheek while the other landed a few inches higher, entering his eye socket and exiting out the other side of his head.

He crumpled to the ground the same as his comrades.

When Bear swung his gun back to where Adams had been standing, he was only met with air.

37

Bear wanted to take off after the Vice President, but Cara took that exact moment to moan and start coming to. Tears rolled down her face, mixing with the blood and dirt to create a muddy mess. She tried to move, but when she jostled her arm, she cried out in pain.

Bear knelt beside her. "Don't move, okay? I'm going to untie you, but you'll have to stay still."

Cara nodded, the tears flowing more freely now. Bear didn't know what to say. I'm sorry? I told you so? You'll be fine? None of those felt right and none of them were fitting. He was sorry for what had happened to her, but she had also chosen to walk down this path. He was proud of her for hunting the truth. He was sure she'd be fine on the outside, but the truth of the matter was that her life was forever changed now.

Bear heard a commotion down the stairs the way Adams had retreated. He pulled his gun back out. "I'm going to be right back, okay? Stay here. Don't move."

Cara looked scared, but Bear liked to believe they had been

through enough together that if he told her he'd be back, she'd believe him.

Bear strode toward the stairs, keeping his gun level. He assumed Jack and Sadie had taken out the rest of the men on the second floor, but there was always the chance that one had gotten away. And he still hadn't cleared the top floor, though it seemed unlikely there were any stragglers up there since no one had come to their boss' aid.

Bear descended the stairs quickly. When he hit the landing, he checked the second floor. The room was filled with bodies, but none of them were Jack or Sadie, so he kept moving.

As he made his way back down to the first floor, he spotted Sadie on the ground, sitting up against the wall. He took the rest of the stairs down two at a time and knelt by her side.

"What happened?"

"Adams came down on my side. Tried to grab him, but he shoved me down the stairs. Jumped over me and went out the door. Jack went after him."

"Are you okay?"

"Fine." Sadie sounded disappointed in herself. She held up one of her elbows. "Couple bruises, but nothing to worry about."

Bear stood to follow Jack just as he came back through the door. The look on his face said everything.

"He got away." Jack banged his fist against the wall. "Took one of the SUVs and drove off."

"It's my fault," Bear said. "I had my gun on him, but he would've killed the girl."

Sadie reached for Bear's outstretched arm and stood up with a groan. "It's no one's fault, okay? We all could've done something differently."

Jack looked at Bear. "We need a new plan."

"I want to help."

Bear turned to see Cara standing at the top of the stairs, holding her broken arm in place. Her left eye was already swollen, but she had managed to wipe some of the blood off her face. She looked like she'd been through the ringer, but she still stood tall.

Bear waited until Jack had helped her down the stairs. They were face-to-face now and he could see the resolution in the young reporter's eyes. There would be no convincing her to stay behind.

"Tell us everything that happened since the hotel room."

Cara backed up a few feet, leaning up against the wall. She winced when she made contact but adjusted and looked at each of them in turn. It looked like it was hard for her to swallow, but she did. When she spoke, her voice was raspy.

"I decided to try to sleep a little more, but I was having trouble. Kept going in and out. I heard the door click open and assumed I'd been out longer than I'd realized. But when I sat up, none of you guys walked through the door."

"Do you know who it was?" Jack asked.

Cara shook her head and then had to steady herself before she continued. "One of them was dead up there on the third floor. I assume the other one is, too."

"What happened next?" Bear asked.

"They had guns. Told me to come with them. If I tried to scream or run, they'd kill everyone and take me anyway. I was so scared. I didn't know what to do."

"It's okay," Sadie said. "You made the right choice."

"You're alive," Bear said. "That's what matters."

"They put me in a black SUV. Vice President Adams was in there. I was so confused. I asked him what was going on, why he had his men point their guns at me. He said they shouldn't have done that. He said they were all on edge because of everything going on."

"He was lying," Bear said.

"I kind of figured that part out on my own." Cara offered a half-smile. "He made it out to seem like Hughes was deranged, like he'd finally gone off the deep end. He said it was time to gather everything we had. He said I made the right call reaching out through the paper, and then asked where I was keeping all the information I had."

"What did you tell him?"

"The truth. I said I had notebooks full of information and I had witnesses. He asked who. I didn't want to tell him. He was insistent. Something felt off. He started to get angry. He hit me and then told the driver to take us somewhere else."

"Here?" Bear asked.

Cara nodded. "We pulled up here along with a couple other cars. Went inside. He took me right up to the third floor and tied me down. Then he left. One of his men was interrogating me, but he must've been told not to touch me because he just kept asking me the same things over and over again. I didn't tell them anything."

"When did they start hitting you?"

"When Adams came back, he was pissed. I heard him say something about how Hughes was dead. I thought maybe it was a good thing, but he seemed even angrier than before. He said he'd kill me if I didn't tell him where he could find you and Jack. I told him I didn't know."

"He obviously didn't believe you."

Cara shook her head again and lost her balance in the process. Sadie grabbed for her to keep her upright and hit her arm. Cara stifled a groan. Fresh tears fell from her eyes.

Sadie turned to Bear. "She needs a hospital."

Cara took a deep breath. Her eyes were still closed, but her voice was stronger than before. "I want to help."

"And you will," Bear said.

Sadie scowled at him. "She needs—"

"A hospital, I know." Bear ran a hand down his face. "But we have to get ahead of this before Adams makes another move. If he blows those tankers in the Gulf, he'll hold all the cards. No one will listen to us if we've got a war on our hands."

Jack crossed his arms. "So, what's the play, Big Man?"

Bear looked from Cara to Sadie and then to Jack. "Call Brandon. We can still track Adams. We need to figure out what he's doing and what his next move is."

"I can make some phone calls, too," Sadie said.

"No, we need you to deal with the tankers in the Gulf. You said the CIA was looking into it, right? Brandon has those emails from Hughes' computer. They talked about a lot. There's gotta be something in there we can use."

Cara stood up a little straighter. "And me?"

"I'm taking you to the hospital."

All three of them started talking at once.

"I want to help—"

"You'll be recognized—"

"It's too dangerous—"

Bear held up his hands. "Cara's at the center of this. She's a civilian. The public is going to believe her more than they'll believe a government agent or a couple guys who used to do the government's bidding. We need to get her in front of a camera." He turned to the young reporter. "But first we need to make sure you're healthy enough to do that."

Jack and Sadie exchanged a look but didn't argue. Cara pushed off the wall and grimaced.

"Okay. Let's do this."

38

BEAR SAT IN THE WAITING AREA OF THE EMERGENCY ROOM. HE SAT perfectly still, but his nerves were wired, and his brain was working overtime. It was more than just feeling trapped. It was like there was a spotlight shining down on him. His body wanted to be on the move, but his brain was forcing him to stay put.

A few hours ago, Jack and Sadie had dropped Bear and Cara off at the entrance to the hospital. They'd driven away to do what they could to take the next step while Bear took Cara under one arm and led her inside. It must've been a quiet day in D.C. because as soon as they walked through the door, two nurses were already there to take Cara away.

They asked Bear what had happened. He didn't know what to say. It was a complicated question and every answer might have implications. The nurses had turned to Cara, who simply said someone had beaten her up.

Then she had looked up at Bear and said, "He saved me."

That was good enough for the nurses. They took her through a heavy door, and when Bear tried to follow, they had told him to stay put. When he tried to ignore them, a burly nurse half his height had poked him in the chest and told him they'd call security if he didn't fall in line.

He backed away after that.

The last thing Cara needed was another complication, and there was no way he was letting himself get kicked out by security.

So instead Bear sat in the same chair for the next few hours. He fell into an easy routine. He looked at his phone, checking for a message from Jack. When he saw there was none, he'd go get a cup of water and bring it back to his seat. He'd check the phone again, and then go get a cup of coffee. When he finished that, he started all over again.

It wasn't much, but it was enough to keep him occupied.

The same burly nurse fetched him as they were creeping up on hour four. The sun was rising and Bear was starting to feel the effects of no sleep despite consuming enough coffee to power a truck. As soon as he saw that nurse, he was awake again. She gave him a look that said, loud and clear, *Don't cause any trouble, buster*, and then led him into the back.

Cara was in a room down the hall and to the right. Her injuries were severe compared to most of the other patients back there, but Bear had passed a room where one guy was getting his face stitched back on. At least Cara didn't have to endure that.

The nurse gestured Bear into the room and then walked away. He paused in the doorway, unsure that she even wanted to see him after everything they'd been through, but he knocked lightly and entered anyway. If nothing else, he wanted to make sure she knew he hadn't abandoned her.

Cara was in bed with one arm in a sling and a swath of gauze across her forehead. She was hooked up to bag of what Bear assumed was saline solution. Other than the bruises on her face, she looked better. Her skin was flush and her eyes were bright.

"Hey," he said.

"Hey."

"How're you feeling?"

"Better." She sat up a little and winced. "Sore. My arm is killing me. But otherwise I'm okay."

Bear gestured vaguely at her. "What's the damage?"

"Mild concussion, separated shoulder, broken arm, cracked rib, and a lot of bruising. Believe it or not, they managed not to break my nose, so I'll still have my good looks after this."

"Looks are overrated," Bear said. "Just look at me."

She laughed and immediately winced.

"Sorry," he said.

"No, it's good to laugh. Even if it hurts. I've been scared out of my mind for days on end. Laughter is exactly what I need right now."

"Sorry about that." When Cara raised her eyebrow at him, Bear continued. "About everything that's happened. I'm sorry I couldn't keep you safe."

Cara rolled her eyes. "Are you kidding? I'd be dead without you, Bear. Literally. You saved my life so many times. I'd rather be scared than dead."

Bear couldn't help but laugh. "That's a good attitude to have."

"Seriously, thank you."

"You don't have to thank me."

"Actually, I do. And I did."

"You're welcome." Bear didn't want to ruin the moment, but he'd always been honest with her. "But we're not out of the woods yet."

"Have you heard from the others yet?"

He shook his head. "They're not going to call until they have something solid."

"Do you think there's even a possibility that we catch him?"

"Oh, yeah." Bear infused his voice with more confidence than he felt. "He's scared now. We've got him on the run."

Cara lowered her voice to a whisper. "Where does the Vice President of the United States run to?"

"U.S. Naval Observatory, maybe. Back to his office in the White House, probably. Wherever he feels safest." Bear took a seat at the end of her bed. "He knows we can't touch him there. He's surrounded by people who are either on his side or who he can manipulate to see things his way."

"And we're just sitting here in a hospital a stone's throw away from him."

Bear shrugged. "It's been a few days since our pictures have circulated. Sadie's done the best she can to shut it down as much as possible. Brandon is keeping an eye out for us. Besides, not taking you to a hospital wasn't really an option."

"I appreciate it." Cara shifted, winced, and settled back into her pillows. "I just want all of this to be over with."

"It will be soon." Bear held himself back from saying *one way or another*. "What's in the cards for you after this?"

Cara laughed. "I don't know. A book deal?"

Bear chuckled. "You're not wrong."

"I kind of just want to go back to my life. But if we take down the VP, I don't think that's a possibility."

"Probably not."

Cara's eyes steeled with resolution. "Then I'll keep doing what I'm doing. And I'll use my platform to keep holding people accountable for their actions."

It was a noble mission. Bear was enough of a cynic that if he heard most people say that, he wouldn't believe them. But there was something about Cara. Something pure and driven. If anyone could save the world one word at a time, he was sure it would be her.

Cara looked over at him. "I'm not going to see you again after this, am I?"

"Never say never." Bear refused to break eye contact. "But it's probably better if that's the case."

"I figured." Cara looked up at the ceiling. "Believe it or not, I think I'm kind of going to miss you."

Bear wasn't sure what to say, so he let her words hang in the air.

"What about you?" she asked. "What are you going to do after all this?"

"Probably disappear for a while. Let things calm down. Maybe go overseas where my picture hasn't been on every television screen for the last few days."

"That sounds smart."

Bear shrugged. It was necessary. But part of him didn't want to think that far ahead. This situation with Adams was too big. Once it was resolved, then he could think of the future. Then he could worry about what was next. A vacation wasn't really in the cards for him, but he did relish the idea of finding another island and drinking beer until he got antsy once more. He wondered if Jack would join him this time or if he'd find somewhere else to go again.

"Speak of the devil," Bear said, fishing his buzzing phone out of his pocket. "Looks like we finally have some news."

39

"I don't like it."

"It doesn't matter how many times you say it, Big Man. Doesn't change what's happening."

Bear crossed his arms over his chest but didn't argue with Jack. They were in a cheap motel room outside of the city. Jack occupied the chair next to the window while Bear leaned up against the headboard, one foot on the ground like he was ready to move at a moment's notice.

They were watching the news, which had been running regular stories all morning up until about twenty minutes ago. Now they were live. The Vice President had called for a press conference, gathering the White House correspondence reporters together for a briefing in the press room. The official story was that he would be making comments about the attacks in London and Germany.

Brandon and Sadie's contacts had figured out he intended to be in front of the cameras right when the tankers blew up.

The whole thing was a PR stunt. If he was calm in the face of chaos, it would go a long way for his own presidential bid down the line. Bear wished he had been shocked by this information but knowing that the government had always employed subtle manipulation to make the general public feel safe or outraged or fearful, depending on what they needed from them, it was nothing new to him.

The plan he and the others had devised was simple. Sadie had used her extensive contacts to go as far up the chain of command as possible. She eventually got five minutes with the President of the United States himself. Those five minutes turned into three hours of discussion and, eventually, a SEAL team headed to the Gulf.

While Vice President Eli Adams expected to be heralded a hero in front of the entire country—the entire world—Jack, Bear, Sadie, and Cara were ready to expose him for the terrorist that he was.

Bear shifted on the bed. Cara was their linchpin in all of this. Sadie had gotten Cara credentials to attend the briefing. She was using a different name, but once Adams saw who it was, Bear bet the shock of seeing her would have its intended effect.

Bear kept reminding himself that she was safe there, surrounded by men that the President had deemed loyal to him alone. But it didn't make Bear feel any better. It had only been a few days since he'd met her, but Cara Bishop had left an impression. After everything she had gone through, she still wanted to be the one to stand face-to-face with Adams and bring him to his knees.

Sadie had volunteered. Out of the four of them, she was the best candidate to get into the White House without raising suspicion, stand up to the Vice President, and announce his wrongdoings on national television.

But Cara had been insistent. It had to come from her.

Bear didn't argue—much. It was the right call. Her still being alive, her being there at the White House, it would unnerve him. If they could throw him off by just a few degrees, it would be enough to get under his skin. And once that seed was planted, it would grow quickly.

Jack cleared his throat. "It's starting soon."

Bear snapped back to focus. It was hard being this far away from the action, his hands completely tied, but both he and Jack had decided it was for the best. Jack was one of the most wanted men in America right now, and Bear had been no slouch over the last couple weeks. It was better if they didn't try to walk through the front door of the White House.

"I still can't believe he's letting us do this," Bear said.

"Who, the President?" Jack shrugged. "This is going to be a PR disaster either way. He knew he couldn't cover it up. The next best scenario is controlling the narrative as much as possible. But we really have to nail Adams to the wall."

"She'll come through," Bear said. Of that, he was certain.

Jack turned his attention to Bear. "Did you talk to her?"

"About what?"

"About how much her life is going to change after this?"

Bear laughed. "She knows. She joked about getting a book deal."

Jack shook his head but there was a smile on his face. "She'll never be able to work as an undercover reporter after this."

"I think she's had enough action for one lifetime." Bear turned back to the TV, searching the crowd of reporters for the back of Cara's head. He got a glimpse of her in the back row before the camera panned away. "Any word from Sadie?"

"She said everything's in place. She and Cara had no problem getting in and getting settled. The team is likely making their move right now. As soon as its over and the tankers are secured, they'll call it in. Sadie said she's got a ringer."

"Did she say what it was?"

Jack rolled his eyes. "No. She said it'd ruin the surprise."

"I've had enough surprises in the last week to last me a lifetime."

"Try telling her that."

"No, thank you."

"Exactly."

Bear turned up the volume on the cheap tv that sat on the dresser across the room. There were only two minutes left now. This was going to be a mess no matter how it played out. The President would have to do some major damage control after this, but he had ensured Sadie that both Jack and Bear would be cleared of all crimes. The files bearing the incidents in Costa Rica, Korea, London, Germany, and here at home would be buried.

There was no such thing as a clean slate, but the President of the United States was offering them what he could. Bear hoped it was enough.

"Ladies and gentleman, the Vice President of the United States."

The reporter's voice corresponded with Adams' entry before the sound from the press room faded in and took over. Adams walked in like he didn't have a care in the world. The smug smile on his face was enough to boil Bear's blood.

But he felt himself calm almost immediately. In a few minutes, nothing else would matter but watching Cara Bishop dismantle this man's entire world brick by brick until he had nothing left to claim as his own except the inside of a jail cell.

40

"GOOD MORNING, EVERYONE."

Adams stood at the podium, a handful of cue cards in front of him. Bear watched him through the television screen, wishing he could be in the room with everyone else when it all came crashing down. Normally he liked his final stands to be on high ground and with an arsenal at his back, but Bear thought the anticipation of watching Adams fall from grace was just as euphoric, even if it was from a distance.

"Thank you for joining me here today," Adams continued. "I have called this press conference because I wanted to talk to you about recent global events. If you have been watching the news, you are aware that the United States and her allies are under attack."

Adams sobered at this point, and Bear couldn't help but wonder how difficult it was for him to keep his glee in check. All eyes were on him. It was exactly what he wanted.

"Unfortunately, I cannot share too much information at this

time, as several of our intelligence agencies are carrying out active investigations into recent events. Many of you may not know about the London bombing because it didn't happen. Due to the efforts of a combined taskforce of American and British operatives, we were able to successfully stop an attack on the underground beneath the city's streets.

"Due to the nature of that operation, I cannot thank those operatives by name, but I hope they are watching this briefing and know how much their efforts are appreciated. They are the unsung heroes of our country, and they will forever be remembered for what they have done in service to both the United States and the United Kingdom."

Bear let out a snort. There was nothing like watching the man who had set the attack in motion thanking those who had put their lives on the line to stop it.

Adams moved one of his cards to the bottom of the pile before he continued. "Just under a week ago, we were unable to prevent a similar terrorist attack that took place during Oktoberfest in Munich, Germany. Several Americans were injured or killed in the explosion in addition to many others from around the globe."

The Vice President shifted from one foot to the other. It had the added effect of displaying his anger and disappointment at his following words. "I regretfully admit we had no information about this attack prior to its being carried out. However, the United States is not in the habit of admitting defeat, and we will not do so here. Since the attack in Germany, we have been more vigilant than ever. In fact, as many of you are probably wondering, that is why I am here delivering this press briefing to you today instead of the Secretary of Defense or the Director of National Intelligence or the President, who is currently acting to ensure the safety of our country and her allies.

"Most of the information I have is, unfortunately, classified. I will not be able to answer specific questions regarding the nature of our investigation, as we do not want to compromise the efforts of all the people who are working around the clock to ensure nobody else dies at the hands of these terrorists.

"Now, I understand that you all want more information and that many people are worried about the safety of their families, both here at home and overseas. Regardless, I will attempt to answer any questions to the best of—"

"Mr. Vice President, how is the Director of National Intelligence?"

Bear's stomach clenched when he heard Cara's voice ring out. There was a murmur in the room. Some of the reporters looked confused, while others seemed annoyed that she had not followed protocol by waiting to be called on.

"I'm sorry." Adams' voice was a mixture of confusion and annoyance. Bear watched as he tried to stay composed while searching for the source of the voice. "Who's speaking?"

"Oh, I'm sorry. The bruises on my face probably make it difficult for you to recognize me."

The cameras all turned to Cara. Her face was a splash of yellows, greens, and purples, and her right arm was in a sling. But despite her outward appearance, Bear could feel her power through the television. She had insisted on being the one to confront her captor, and though Bear had voiced his opposition to this plan in the beginning, he had to admit it had the intended effect.

"My name is Cara Bishop. Yes, I'm the reporter who was falsely accused of the murder of billionaire Thomas Mateo. I am also the reporter who wrote the op-ed for the *Tribune* discussing a grand conspiracy within the ranks of our government."

Adams leaned closer, his face a perfect mask of confusion. "I'm sorry, I don't know—"

"Let's stop playing games, Mr. Vice President. You were, after all, my contact in the White House. I wrote the article for you. It was our signal to get in touch with each other. To move forward with our plan. To expose those who were behind this grand conspiracy. Who were, as a matter of fact, also behind these global acts of terrorism, you have been speaking about today. So, I'll ask again: How is the Director of National Intelligence?"

"You are disrupting this press briefing. I will kindly ask you to leave before I am forced to have you escorted out."

Cara was the pinnacle of strength as she made her way down her row of reporters and toward the center aisle, where she stood alone against the Vice President. "The last I heard, he was dead, but no formal announcement has been made. I wonder why? Why is that being kept under wraps? Is it because you don't know who killed him? Or is it because you *do*?"

Murmurs erupted within the press room. Adams turned to the guards lining the wall. "Please escort her out of here."

None of them moved.

"There's another reason why you might know who I am." Cara's voice faltered for the first time, but only slightly. To Bear it didn't sound like fear. It sounded like anger. "I'm the one your men held at gunpoint. I'm the one your men beat for information. I'm okay, by the way, though you didn't ask. I have a cracked rib. Makes it hard to breathe sometimes. A mild concussion. They say I should be okay. There's no swelling. The bruises will fade. The scrapes will heal. The shoulder—that's a different story. It'll be fine, but it won't ever be quite the same."

Cara took three steps forward. She had the command of the entire room. Even Adams was enthralled. He couldn't look away, even though Bear was certain he was thinking of every possible exit scenario he had ever devised.

"You know, someone asked me the other day, *What will you do after this?*" She laughed quietly. "I still only had one, single thought: I was going to be a reporter. This wasn't going to stop me. Did you know this was my first story? At least it was the first one of consequence.

"What I can't wrap my head around is why you helped me for so long. And then this morning it came to me. You wanted to control the narrative. That's why you're holding this press briefing, isn't it? You want to make sure the world sees only what you want it to see. You're expecting some man in a uniform to walk up to you and whisper something into your ear. That something would have been another terrorist attack. This time, it would've been an explosion of tankers in the Persian Gulf. If it had been successful, what would've been next? An attack on the United States? Would you have urged the President to declare war before or after? How long would you have let this continue before convincing the government to occupy the Middle East, bringing its people and resources under our control for good?"

At this point, Adams was speechless. He was looking around at the men in uniform who surrounded him, beseeching them with his eyes to do something, *anything*.

One of the men did step forward. Bear didn't recognize him, but he wore his dress uniform with his hat held under one arm. For the briefest of minutes, the Vice President looked relieved. And then the man spoke.

"My name is Lieutenant General Andrew Gibson. The Vice President thinks I'm here to deliver him a piece of intelligence indicating that several tankers in the Persian Gulf have been attacked by a group of unknown terrorists. Instead, I'm here to report that the threat has been thwarted and the tankers remain in one piece. Unfortunately, I am also here to confess my knowledge of and involvement in both the London and Munich bombings."

When the man turned toward Cara, his face softened. "You don't know me, Ms. Bishop, but I've been following your story for quite some time. When your picture was first shown on the news, I had a hard time believing you were a killer. I was with my daughter at the time. She was still recovering in the hospital from the bomb that went off in Germany. I had been stationed there and didn't know she'd snuck away to go to the Oktoberfest celebrations."

Bear sat up a little straighter.

"Her name is Amber Gibson. She almost died that day, but thanks to a man named Riley Logan, she walked away with a broken leg and second-degree burns on her arm. She's alive because of him. I know I'll never be able to thank him for that, so I thought I'd do the next best thing."

Gibson turned back to Adams. "The Vice President and I don't know each other well. I worked with the Director of National Intelligence for many years. We were in the army together, and though we went our separate ways, we stayed in touch. A few years ago, he invited me out for a drink. We got to talking about the state of this country. About the state of the world.

"I, like Director Hughes, believed we needed to do more to secure our place in this world. I wanted to keep the people of this country safe. I wanted to keep my daughter safe." Gibson paused to gather himself. "Except she was there, in Germany. And one of the men who is accused of these terrorist attacks saved her life. He comforted her when I couldn't. And I do not regret to inform you that I can no longer abide by your plan, Mr. Vice President. I will take the consequences deemed necessary for the crimes I have committed, and I will apologize to this country, to our President, and most importantly, to my daughter, for betraying all of your trust. But I will take it, happily and gladly, knowing, Mr. Vice President, that you will be in a jail cell next to mine."

It seemed as though the room was collectively holding its breath. All eyes were on Gibson until Cara once again stepped forward. She looked Adams dead in the eyes.

"I think that about covers our press briefing for today, don't you?"

41

"WHERE DID YOU FIND HIM?"

"Believe it or not, he found us."

Bear, Sadie, and Jack sat around a table in some hole-in-the-wall pub in downtown Washington D.C., drinking beer and decompressing after what felt like a lifetime of lies and conspiracies and accusations.

Sadie slugged back the rest of her beer and set the bottle down with a *clunk*. "Between the op-ed that Cara wrote and seeing your face on television, Gibson had pieced together the information Hughes and Adams had been keeping from him. He knew we worked together in London, so he found me. He was a mess."

"He's got a good kid." Bear remembered the way she'd pushed through her fear and pain. Her father would've been proud of her. "I hope she'll be okay."

Sadie shrugged. "Gibson did a lot of things wrong, but I have a feeling his confession will go a long way in redeeming him in her eyes. And hopefully the courts will see that, too. He might not end up spending the rest of his life in a jail cell."

"Adams on the other hand…"

The fallout from the press conference had been immediate. Even a week later, the news cycle hadn't let anyone forget that the Vice President of the United States had betrayed his country. The President had issued a statement, but they were keeping most of the information regarding Hughes and Adams' plan under wraps. The less the general public knew, the better. But this was certainly a hit for the administration.

Sadie stood up and slipped on her winter jacket. "I should probably get going."

"Already?" Jack looked at his watch. "It's a little early, isn't it?"

"I've got to go in early tomorrow. For some reason, when they said they were giving me a promotion, I figured I'd get paid more to do less work. You know, like every boss I've ever had. Turns out that isn't the case."

"Any idea where they're sending you first?"

"Nope, but I hope it's somewhere warm. I'm already tired of this weather." She leaned over and gave Bear a hug, holding on for a fraction longer than was customary. When she straightened up, she had a sad smile on her face. She turned to Jack. "Walk me out?"

Jack got up wordlessly, thumping Bear on the back and following Sadie out of the bar. Bear watched them go and then ordered another round. The waitress brought another couple of bottles to the table and cleared the empty ones. Before she walked away, she put a hand on her hip and looked him up and down.

"I feel like I know you from somewhere."

"I've just got one of those faces."

She shrugged and returned to the bar, but Bear saw her cast a glance at him every so often. He turned his back on her, hiding his face.

Bear scratched at his beard. Cara had suggested—again—

that Bear shave it off. No one would recognize him, she'd insisted, but he couldn't bring himself to do it. Besides, it had already been a week and it felt like most people had moved on. He and Jack had been given a presidential pardon, and for now, everyone's attention was on the Vice President's crimes and his eventual trial.

In a few more weeks, or maybe a month or two, Jack and Bear would be just another face in the crowd.

Bear took a healthy pull of his beer and thought about Cara. He'd had a chance to say goodbye to her, though it had been brief. She'd hugged him, and thanked him once again, but he'd shrugged it off. She'd done her part in all of this, and if it hadn't been for her and Gibson's public appearances, Bear would probably be locked up right alongside Adams.

But he had his freedom. He wasn't sure what he was going to do with it yet, but that would be a problem for a later date. For now, he was content to see where the world took him. But wherever he was, he knew he'd check up on Cara Bishop every once in a while, just to make sure she hadn't gotten into any more trouble.

And to make sure she got that book deal.

Jack returned a few minutes later, bringing the December chill back with him. He downed half his beer and shook his head.

"What?" Bear asked.

"I don't know, man." He shook his head again. "I don't know."

"You think Sadie's going to be okay?"

Jack laughed. "She's going to be fine."

"What about you?"

"I'll be fine, too." Jack paused and took another pull of his beer. "But I'm not going to lie, it's been nice having her around."

Bear felt the same way. There was something comforting about knowing Sadie had your back. It was more than just the fact that she was an incredible operative. She was also just a good friend.

Jack and Bear didn't have too many of those. Associates? Yes. Contacts? Definitely. But friends?

They could count those on one hand.

"We'll see her again."

"Oh, I'm sure of that." Jack laughed. "Probably when we have a half dozen guns to our heads."

"She would choose that exact moment to show up and ream us out for not calling her."

Jack's laugh echoed around the bar. A few people turned in their direction.

"I missed this," Jack said. "Being in the same place. Drinking a couple beers."

"Not getting shot at."

"Or blown up."

It was Bear's turn to laugh. "Especially that one."

"We make a pretty good team, Big Man." Jack held up his bottle.

Bear clinked his drink to Jack's. "Maybe we should stick together for a while this time."

"Fine by me." Jack leaned back against the wall and surveyed the bar. "But what should we do next? I feel like we've really peaked with this last mission of ours. You don't get much bigger than accusing the Vice President of the United States of global terrorism."

"You're not wrong." Bear finished off his beer. "Maybe we should lay low for a while."

Jack scoffed. "What's the fun in that?"

Just then, his cell phone rang. Jack pulled it out of his jacket pocket and looked down at the number. His eyebrows knit together.

"Who is it?"

Jack shrugged and opened the phone, holding it to his head. "Hello?"

Bear could hear a muffled voice on the other end, but he couldn't tell who it was. He couldn't even tell if it was a man or woman. Not many people had Jack's number, and those that didn't have it would have to go through hell to get it.

Jack's eyes met Bear's, but Bear couldn't read his expression. He was still processing the information.

"Okay," Jack said. "We'll meet you there soon."

Bear rolled his eyes as Jack hung up the phone. "You just had to go and say something, didn't you?"

Jack shrugged. "You didn't think the universe wasn't going to let us off the hook that easily, did you?"

"I had hope." Bear threw a wad of ones down on the table. "We're due for a break sooner rather than later."

Jack stood up and stretched, clapping Bear on the back.

"Looks like it's going to be later, Big Man."

ALSO BY L.T. RYAN

Into The Darkness

Deliver Us From Darkness - coming soon

Affliction Z Series

Affliction Z: Patient Zero

Affliction Z: Abandoned Hope

Affliction Z: Descended in Blood

Affliction Z Book 4 - Spring 2018

ABOUT THE AUTHOR

L.T. Ryan is a *USA Today* and international bestselling author. The new age of publishing offered L.T. the opportunity to blend his passions for creating, marketing, and technology to reach audiences with his popular Jack Noble series.

Living in central Virginia with his wife, the youngest of his three daughters, and their three dogs, L.T. enjoys staring out his window at the trees and mountains while he should be writing, as well as reading, hiking, running, and playing with gadgets. See what he's up to at http://ltryan.com.

Social Medial Links:

- Facebook (L.T. Ryan): https://www.facebook.com/LTRyanAuthor

- Facebook (Jack Noble Page): https://www.facebook.com/JackNobleBooks/

- Twitter: https://twitter.com/LTRyanWrites

- Goodreads: http://www.goodreads.com/author/show/6151659.L_T_Ryan

Made in the USA
Columbia, SC
06 January 2025

51253182R00157